W9-AMA-929

"What do you think you're doing, Julien?"

"Me? I'm walking you to work. Kind of romantic, don't you think?"

"Why aren't you at work?"

"I was, before the sun came up. I stopped in to have a late breakfast and you…were missing."

"So you tracked me down and embarrassed me yet again?"

She trotted off at a fast pace, but felt his hand warm on her arm. "I don't want to embarrass you."

"Then what do you call this?"

Julien leaned close, his dark eyes holding hers. "I call this making up for lost time. I'm yours, Alma. And I believe it's time we both get used to that idea."

Alma's shock caused her to gasp. "Mine? You were never mine. And I'll never be yours. You might have considered that before you decided to launch an attack on me."

"I'm not attacking, darlin'," he said on a whisper. "I'm wooing. I want to make you mine."

Books by Lenora Worth

Love Inspired

†*The Carpenter's Wife*
†*Heart of Stone*
†*A Tender Touch*
Blessed Bouquets
  "The Dream Man"
*A Certain Hope
*A Perfect Love
*A Leap of Faith
Christmas Homecoming
Mountain Sanctuary
Lone Star Secret
Gift of Wonder
The Perfect Gift
Hometown Princess
Hometown Sweetheart
The Doctor's Family
Sweetheart Reunion

Love Inspired Suspense

A Face in the Shadows
Heart of the Night
Code of Honor
Risky Reunion
Assignment: Bodyguard
The Soldier's Mission
Body of Evidence

Steeple Hill

After the Storm
Echoes of Danger
Once Upon a Christmas
  "'Twas the Week Before
  Christmas"

†Sunset Island
*Texas Hearts

LENORA WORTH

has written more than forty books for three different publishers. Her career with Love Inspired Books spans close to fifteen years. In February 2011 her Love Inspired Suspense novel *Body of Evidence* made the *New York Times* bestseller list. Her very first Love Inspired title, *The Wedding Quilt,* won *Affaire de Coeur*'s Best Inspirational for 1997, and *Logan's Child* won an *RT Book Reviews* Best Love Inspired for 1998. With millions of books in print, Lenora continues to write for the Love Inspired and Love Inspired Suspense lines. For years Lenora also wrote a weekly opinion column for the local paper and worked freelance with a local magazine. She has now turned to full-time fiction writing and enjoying adventures with her retired husband, Don. Married for thirty-six years, they have two grown children. Lenora enjoys writing, reading and shopping…especially shoe shopping.

Sweetheart Reunion
Lenora Worth

Love Inspired

If you purchased this book without a cover you should be aware that this book is stolen property. It was reported as "unsold and destroyed" to the publisher, and neither the author nor the publisher has received any payment for this "stripped book."

Recycling programs for this product may not exist in your area.

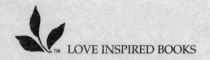

™ LOVE INSPIRED BOOKS

ISBN-13: 978-0-373-81614-9

SWEETHEART REUNION

Copyright © 2012 by Lenora H. Nazworth

All rights reserved. Except for use in any review, the reproduction or utilization of this work in whole or in part in any form by any electronic, mechanical or other means, now known or hereafter invented, including xerography, photocopying and recording, or in any information storage or retrieval system, is forbidden without the written permission of the editorial office, Love Inspired Books, 233 Broadway, New York, NY 10279 U.S.A.

This is a work of fiction. Names, characters, places and incidents are either the product of the author's imagination or are used fictitiously, and any resemblance to actual persons, living or dead, business establishments, events or locales is entirely coincidental.

This edition published by arrangement with Love Inspired Books.

® and TM are trademarks of Love Inspired Books, used under license. Trademarks indicated with ® are registered in the United States Patent and Trademark Office, the Canadian Trade Marks Office and in other countries.

www.LoveInspiredBooks.com

Printed in U.S.A.

Therefore with joy shall ye
draw water out of the wells of salvation.
—*Isaiah* 12:3

To Jackie Tatum for being a loyal reader and a sweet friend. Thanks to Mary Hymel for answering all my questions about hunting season and a lot of other things in Cajun Country. Any mistakes are my own! And…in memory of Ruth Roach.

Chapter One

Another day, another dollar.

Alma Blanchard stood inside the empty Fleur Bakery and Café, watching the first rays of sunrise crest with all the magnificence of a giant golden shield over the still, lush Louisiana bayou. The scent of fresh-baked bread and crisp bacon filled the air and the long kitchen at the back of the café sizzled and fizzed with morning activity.

She put down her coffee, brushed strands of long dark hair away from her face and steeled herself for the busy morning rush. The old clapboard restaurant echoed with the tap of her sneakers on the aged cypress floors. She'd just turned the key inside the big industrial lock when a face, silhouetted against the slanted rays of the dawn sun, appeared on the other side of the glass paneled doors.

A face she'd just as soon not see so early in the morning.

Julien LeBlanc.

He grinned at her, flashing dimples and dark onyx eyes that always reminded her of a bayou night. Pushing a calloused, tanned hand through his thick dark bangs, he said, "C'mon, *chère*, open up. I'm needing some of that good coffee, for sure."

Alma willed her heart to slow down, wondering why after ten years Julien still had this kind of effect on her. It wasn't as if she still cared about him. Any feelings she'd had for Julien were long dead. But still…memories of high school and Julien hit her with the same intensity he used to tap against the door.

"You're killing me, Alma," he called, his nose pressed to the glass panes. "Please, pretty please."

"Hold on," she called out, twisting the big lock, her hands suddenly clammy, her joyfulness vanished as she stood back to let him in. Grabbing her coffee as a shield, she said, "I'm not awake yet."

Julien muscled his way inside the second the big oak door gave way, the scent of spicy soap and early morning fresh air surrounding him. He stood, hands on his hips, his impish gaze sliding over her like warm, glistening water. Tilting his head low so he could lock his gaze on her, he said, "You look awake to me, darlin'. And as pretty as those morning glories blooming out on the front porch."

Then he took her coffee cup from her and drank deeply. "Ahh, you make the best coffee in south Louisiana."

"Stop it with the charm," Alma said, her tone turned sassy even while her stomach turned sour. They did this, played out this flirting dance, each time they were around each other. She both enjoyed and dreaded it. But it was their shield against the truth. "Just get in here and let me get to work. What do you want, Julien? Besides coffee, that is."

He gave her a look that told her exactly what he wanted. The resigned longing in his eyes reminded her of sweet poetry whispered by the light of a crescent moon. Then the look was gone. "Me, I'm starving. Eggs over hard, bacon, grits and biscuits. Double on all."

"How do you stay in shape?" Alma asked, turning to hurry behind the safety of the long wooden counter.

And why did she ask such stupid questions? The man worked day and night out on his boat, didn't he? And when he wasn't out in the Gulf waters trolling for shrimp or in the bayous working his traps, he was busy building boats. Beautiful one-of-a kind boats. A hard worker, her Julien.

No, not *her* Julien, no matter how hard he tried to flirt with her. No matter the memories of distant times lodged in her brain like a log jam.

He'd never be hers again.

And she'd best remember that.

Besides, she didn't have time to dwell on the past and Julien LeBlanc. Time to open the café to all the other regular customers and the early-bird tourists.

Alma put his order through then disappeared into the kitchen, a fresh *new* cup of dark roast coffee steaming in her hand, while she looked out the big kitchen window in the back of the café and watched a tall white egret spread its wings and lift gracefully out over the dark water. The egret settled like a ballerina near a stand of bald cypress trees covered with Spanish moss then strolled through the shallows, dipping its long beak as it searched for breakfast.

Alma sighed, took a sip of the strong brew and wondered why she felt so out of sorts this morning. Such a beautiful, peaceful beginning to her day. Such a joyful morning. She should have reveled in God's handiwork. All around her, the early crew chatted and fussed, working to get the day started, some singing, some whining. But right here, right now, with the spring day beginning in all its glory and the promise of unexpected gifts in the air, Alma felt alone. Thinking about Julien and what they'd once had didn't help. So she said a little prayer that she would be at peace in God's world.

Just for a minute, Lord.

Mama would have loved this morning, Alma thought, memories of her mother Lila moving with the same grace as the elegant egret. Maybe that was why Alma was so off-kilter. She missed her mother each and every day, but nothing could be done for that. Mama had been dead for almost eight years now. And Alma was still in the same spot, always staring out into the world and wondering if there was something more out there for her.

But Alma had promised her mother she'd keep the café going, so she had bread to bake and meals to cook and supervise. The shrimpers and fishermen and tourists would want a good breakfast this fine spring morning.

And so would Julien.

She grabbed his order and took it out to him. "Here you go. Eat it while it's hot."

"Sit with me a spell," he said, his dark eyes lifting up to her face, his hand touching her arm with a lightness that didn't match the expression on his face.

"You know I have to work." Trying to hide her surprise, she motioned to two regulars sitting nearby. "In case you haven't noticed, you're not the only customer here."

"You work too hard."

"It takes one to know one." She hurried away, her heart beating right along with her sneakers as they hit the old wooden floor. Why did it have to hurt this way each time she was around him?

"Order up," she called, her back to the man who'd broken her heart so long ago. She intended to keep doing what she'd done for the past ten years. She'd be civil to Julien because, in spite of their breakup long ago, they were still friends and besides, he was a loyal customer. A very loyal customer. Nothing new there. Nothing new in her life, either.

Except today he'd touched her and asked her to sit with him. Today, Julien seemed different, more intense, more aware.

That left Alma rattled and disoriented.

Don't give in to that, she told herself. *He's just being charming Julien.*

But she could feel his dark eyes burning through her with the same glaring warmth and intensity as that orb of sunshine lifting out over the cypress trees.

Why did this woman still get to him so much?

Julien swigged his coffee and stabbed at another piece of crisp, crunchy bacon, nodding his head as he pretended to listen to one of his friend Tebow's outrageous tales. He could recite most of Tebow's nonsense chapter and verse. Right now, he'd rather watch Alma at work.

He loved watching Alma, and that was a fact.

Her long curly hair was piled up high on her head, except for a few rebellious chocolate-colored strands that danced around her face and eyes. Today, she wore faded jeans and an old T-shirt underneath a worn white apron that proclaimed in big, bold, red print "Fleur Bakery and Café. So good make you want to slap your mama." The sturdy walking shoes on her feet were white and blue with tiny rhinestones winking across the vamps each time she sashayed by. And each time she did sashay by, Julien caught the scent of a garden, exotic and floral.

Nice. But Julien could still see her back in high school at their senior prom, all dressed up in light-blue silk, looking like a princess who'd gotten lost in the swamp. She'd been his back then and he'd loved her with all the angst and need of an eighteen-year-old teenager.

He was no longer eighteen but he still had that angst. He tried to hide it with flirtations and jokes, but it was like those bayou waters out there, still and calm on the surface but churning with a thousand undercurrents deep in the dark murky places.

Idiot flirt that he was, he'd messed things up by getting into a fight with Alma at the prom and then getting caught later that night with one of her best friends. Too much spiked punch and too many raging hormones had done him in. That and the fear of loving her too much—and losing her to that big-time life away from Fleur she wanted so badly. But his fears had cost him, thanks to his own fatal need to sabotage any chance of happiness. He'd lost the love of his life on the night he'd planned to ask her to marry him.

She'd never forgiven him.

And she never would.

Didn't matter much, since he could never forgive himself either. Didn't matter much that he'd stopped drinking for good last year, but he was too ashamed to tell her that and beg her to take him back. His Alma hadn't gone off to find fame and fortune in some big, lonely city. She'd stayed here to help her family. But she still managed to mostly ignore him. While he came in here every day and smiled at her and tried to forget what they'd once had. Maybe that was his penance.

For that reason, Julien had to pretend he didn't care. Had to pretend he was so over Alma Blanchard. These past few months had been hard on his family. He was tired of pretending. But a man could hope, *oui?* A man could learn from his mistakes and try to piece his life back together, one day at a time. Only now, his little brother seemed to be heading down that same slippery slope. The very thing that had brought Julien's drinking to a skidding halt has caused his brother to take it up right where Julien left off. Their papa had died. Were the LeBlanc men cursed to be self-destructive? Maybe that was why Julien had needed to see Alma's face this morning. He needed a bit of hope.

"Did you hear me?"

Julien glanced over at Tebow. His friend had that look on his face again. That smug look that told Julien he couldn't fool a man who'd known him since they'd both been in diapers.

"Your heart is showing, *mon ami*," Tebow said on a low breath. "'Cause you're wearing it on your sleeve again."

"Shut up," Julien growled, his appetite sated. "Let's get out of here."

"Testy this morning," Tebow said before lopping his worn LSU baseball cap back onto his head. "What, she put you in your place again?"

Julien ignored his friend's ribbing, choosing instead to focus on paying his check. And leaving a big tip. Alma worked hard, cooked the best food in the world and tried to hold her family together. He knew what she'd sacrificed to stay here in Fleur, knew all about her dreams to go to cooking school and become a chef in New Orleans. Or maybe Atlanta. Or had it been New York? Didn't matter now.

He knew what she'd given up all those years ago when, right after he'd broken her heart, her mama had come down with breast cancer and fought it for two years. But she'd never recovered. Healed, but not in this life.

He knew.

And he ached for Alma each and every day. Which was why he always started his day right here in the café.

Just to be near her.

He knew. But if he didn't do something and do it soon, she'd never know that he still loved her.

"I'm starving."

Alma laughed at her older sister Callie's antics, shaking her head as Callie fell across the counter. "Okay, I can take a hint. Let me grab us a couple of sandwiches. You want chicken salad or marinated shrimp?"

"Chicken salad," Callie replied, waving her hands in the air. "And some of those good sweet potato fries. Wanna eat out on the back deck?"

Alma glanced outside. The lunch crowd had died down and the place was quiet, the dark paneled walls and cool hardwood giving it a coziness that made her want to take a long nap. But she didn't have time to nap during the day. And she rarely slept at night.

"I think outside. Tea or coffee?" she called to her golden-haired sister.

"Hmm. Spiced tea. It's getting to be that time of year, you know."

"Spiced tea it is," Alma called over her shoulder. "Go find a table in the shade. I'll bring it out."

Callie spun on the old black vinyl stool then stood to stretch, her worn cotton button-up shirt as deep blue as her expressive eyes. She looked so much like their mother—all gold and sunshine and fiery—but delicate. Callie had survived her own breast cancer scare only to lose her husband. The man couldn't deal with the sickness, so he'd left. Yeah, Callie survived all right, with a broken heart.

Alma didn't intend to ever let that happen to her. Better to focus on work and family, especially on their daddy, Ramon. He'd taken Mama's death hard. They all had. But Ramon Blanchard was never the same after Lila passed away. Alma and Callie kept tabs on him, and their other sister, Brenna, away in Baton Rouge, called him just about every day.

Bringing a tray full of food with her, Alma hit her hip against the old screen door to the covered back porch of the café. The porch, decorated with old car tags and folksy plaques with Cajun sayings and normally full of customers, was mostly quiet during the afternoon hours. Only a few people were left eating a late lunch, then things would start all over again with the second shift and the supper crowd.

"Busy day?" Alma asked after she placed their food on the table and sat down on one of the old high-backed wooden chairs.

Callie nodded, chewing the sandwich Alma had made with fresh sourdough bread. "With this weather, everyone is ready to get back to gardening. Seems to be picking up."

"That's good. It'll keep you out of trouble."

Alma glanced over next door to where her sister spent most of her time. Callie's Corner Nursery did a big business year-round. When she wasn't busy helping customers plant their gardens or redo their landscaping for spring and summer, Callie turned to fall plants and pumpkins, then selling Christmas trees and designing beautiful natural door wreaths during the winter. Her sister worked as hard as Alma did, but they had different talents and passions. Callie was good with her hands and growing things, while Alma loved to cook and bake. Brenna was the civilized, artistic sister. And the one who'd managed to move away.

"Talk to Papa today?" Callie asked between nibbles of sweet potato fries.

"Early this morning, just briefly," Alma responded. "He sounded okay. Had a group of lawyers from up in Shreveport down for some deep sea fishing. Should be back by now, though." She glanced at her watch, wondering if Papa would come by for supper tonight.

Callie tapped a finger on the wooden table. "He'll be okay. He always enjoys taking the boat out."

"I worry about him," Alma said. "I know you do, too."

Callie nabbed another fry. "Yes, but what can we do? Nothing will mend his broken heart."

"No, nothing."

Alma looked out at the bank that fell away from the steps leading down to the bayou. Large live oaks dripping with gray moss shaded the tin-roofed porch. A mockingbird chirped and fussed in one of the live oak's branches. Out near the shallows, palmetto palms and rhododendrons languished on the black, decay-filled earth. Somewhere off in the bushes, a frog croaked a repetitive song. An old log jutting out into the water held two turtles that seemed to be enjoying the warm, filtered sun dappling the dark water.

"What are you thinking?" Callie asked, her blue eyes as deep as the gulf waters just a few miles away.

Alma pushed back in her chair. "Why do you always ask me that?"

"Maybe because you're always thinking."

"I have a brain, therefore I think."

Callie dropped the last of her sandwich then wiped her hands on her napkin. "You get like Papa, all dark and sad, when you look out over that water. Especially after Julien's been around."

"It's not Julien." Alma denied the pain in her heart. "I miss Mama, of course. I guess I sit here and think about what might have been."

Callie glanced at the water then back at Alma. "We all think about that from time to time."

"Do you miss being married?" Alma asked, her pain now for her sister.

Callie shrugged, but her expression hardened against her high cheekbones, causing her face to blush pale. She nodded, dark golden curls shimmying around her face. "I miss what I thought marriage was supposed to be. I wanted what Papa and Mama had. I thought I'd found that with Roy, but I was wrong. If I ever decide to get married again, I want someone with sticking power—the kind that lasts through thick and thin, through sickness and health."

"Just as the vow you spoke promised," Alma said, wishing she hadn't asked the question. "Just like Papa and Mama."

Callie lowered her head. "Yes, just like that."

Then she looked up at Alma. "Is that what you were thinking about, really? Marriage and a family?"

"Not for me," Alma retorted, gathering their empty plates, the image of Julien smiling at her playing through her mind. "Do you want pie?"

Her sister gave her a resigned look. "What kind?"

"Today I have coconut and key lime."

"Can we split a piece of key lime?"

"I don't see why not."

Alma took their dishes in and smiled when Winnie, one of her long-time waitresses, handed her two tiny slivers of key lime pie.

"I heard you ask," Winnie explained. "The door is open after all."

"Is that all you heard?"

Winnie bobbed her head, her brown bob flowing around her face. "Yes, *ma fille,* that's all I heard. I didn't have to hear the rest. I saw that tale told on your faces."

Curious, Alma turned at the screen door, holding the pie plates one in each hand. "And what tale was that?"

"Two sisters, remembering and regretting. That's all."

Winnie turned and went back to her afternoon chores.

Alma turned and went back to her sister.

Winnie was right. Two sisters remembering and regretting, nothing more.

Except the knowing that they might not ever have the kind of marriage their parents had. Callie had learned that the day her husband walked out. Brenna refused to even discuss such nonsense.

Alma had learned the same at a very early age. She'd learned it the night she'd found Julien LeBlanc in the arms of another girl.

Chapter Two

Julien unloaded his catch of the day at the back of the Fleur Bakery, his eyes ever wary but hopeful for the sight of Alma. Wary because he knew she didn't like having him around. Hopeful because he liked seeing her around.

Couldn't be helped, either way, since they did business together. He occasionally provided fresh seafood to her restaurant and she cooked it up into some of the best around. And tonight, he had a few hundred pounds of fresh crawfish from the small farm he worked during the season. It looked to be a good year, even after all the heartache of storms and oil spills.

Julien loved springtime the best. It was a time of renewal and hope, a time when he remembered being young and carefree and in love. Fish jumping, fresh vegetables and fruit growing, swimming holes open and flowing, and long ago, Alma in his arms dancing at the annual spring festival. Lately, however, he didn't seem to enjoy dancing the way he had when he was young and carefree. Nothing was the same without Alma, anyway.

Why had he waited so long to see that, to admit that?

The poet in him wanted to be young and carefree again, wanted that innocence of a first kiss, that newborn hope of a first dance.

He wanted what he'd had with Alma. That realization had hit him like a gale force wind the day they'd buried his daddy last fall. But it had taken him all winter to figure it all out.

The pragmatic side in him knew to quit dreaming and get on with the here and now. His late father's birthday was coming up in a few days. That reminder made Julien less carefree and more somber. That and the fact that his baby brother, Pierre, twenty-one and on a path of self-destruction, needed Julien to be a better role model. No revelation there.

But Julien had managed a few epiphanies lately. He believed in signs, little hints from the Almighty. He didn't have to be hit on the head to get it through his noggin that something in his life needed to change.

Alma walked out the back door, and both of those conflicting sides of him merged into a hopeful regret. Or maybe a regretful hope.

Technically, they'd broken up in high school but Julien had never let go. Besides, they couldn't avoid each other in such a small town. So they'd learned to be polite to each other, and over the years that politeness had aged into a patina of respect and appreciation, along with a rub of regret. He'd always been conflicted around Alma. Now he wanted to start over, all new and improved, and he wanted to win her back.

He smiled up at her now, determined not to show that conflict. Alma could sense turmoil the way an old-timer could predict a storm coming in off the gulf. She had that ability.

"Look, Alma. Got you some big, juicy bugs here." He watched as his grumpy younger brother finished carrying the heavy bags full of still live crawfish into the storage area. Shooting Pierre a hard glance, Julien added, "Gonna be a good night on the bayou."

Alma stood with her hands on her hips, looking for all the world like a pirate queen about to make a man walk the plank. "I reckon those will do just fine. Thank you, Julien."

"Thanks back to you and I'll take my check now." He handed her a receipt, grinning to stop the pain edging through his heart. "You look tired, *chère*. Long day?"

Alma glanced away, irritation marring her pretty face. "It's always a long day around here."

Julien leaned one booted foot up onto the steps. "You work too much. You need to take some time away."

"Since when are you so worried about my work schedule?"

Since he'd had an epiphany or two. But he couldn't explain that to Alma. She worried about his lack of faith. She'd have him by the ear and through the church doors before he could say "Praise the Lord and pass the salt."

So he said, "Since I've seen you in this place mostly every day and night for as long as I can remember."

She fussed with checking his haul. "I get days off every week."

"*Oui,* and you spend them mostly right here."

"How do you know what I do?" Alma asked, her deep-blue eyes crashing like an angry ocean.

"I see you most every day so it's kinda hard to miss," Julien replied, the smile gone out of his words. "I worry for you."

"Don't," she said, tossing hair away from her face. "Just get your load finished so I can get back to my customers."

Something inside of Julien snapped. He'd had a long, hard day, too, and too long of a time thinking about her. And he was proud of his catch. He wanted Alma to be proud of him. Or maybe he just needed Alma to see him, really see him, again. She thought he was heartless, without a soul. But she'd never know how he prayed in the long, silent nights of longing for things he might not ever have. He'd prayed all right. He had faith. He just wasn't one to go shouting it to the world.

"I think you should get away from this kitchen and your customers for a while."

"I have work to do, Julien, so stop thinking and get back to unloading."

"All done." He hopped over the last two steps then said something to his brother in French. Pierre rolled his eyes but nodded then went back to the truck and cranked it.

"Your brother is leaving you," Alma pointed out, nodding toward the roaring pickup.

"I told him to go on home," Julien said, taking her by the hand. Then he turned to the window into the kitchen. "Miss Alma is taking a little break. Winnie, you can keep everyone happy for a while, can't you?"

Winnie grinned into the window, her brown bangs flipped over the crinkles in her eyes. "*Oui!* Take your time."

Alma pulled away. "Since when do you go ordering my staff around, Julien LeBlanc?"

He grabbed her hand and held tight. "Since you look like you're about to fall out. Since you need to rest but you won't do it. Since…just now when I decided to take matters into my own hands."

Alma held back, glancing through the window to frown at the still grinning Winnie. "I don't have time for your foolishness. I have people—"

"Who can cook and clean and smile at other people while you take a walk with me along the bayou. Five minutes, Alma. That's all I ask."

Alma stared down at his hand in hers, wondering why his big, tanned fingers seemed to fit so closely to her own work-worn hands. And wondering why she just wanted to sit down and have a nice little cry. Why did she feel as if she'd missed out on something important?

Pushing that idea aside, she tried once again to pull away. "Julien, I'm fine. I can't go for a walk during suppertime."

He didn't let go. "Yes, you can. C'mon. It's a nice evening."

She couldn't argue with that. A cool spring breeze played through the bald cypress trees lining the banks, the gray-beard moss swaying against the branches like old lace falling against leather. A flock of brown pelicans flew by, the symmetry of their wings lifted high up in the sky in perfect formation over the water. The sight was as natural to her way of life as breathing. Scenes such as this normally brought her a certain calm. But with Julien nearby, her heart spurted like a burned-out boat motor.

Sighing, Alma followed Julien down the steps in spite of the need for self-control shouting in her head. "Five minutes, then I have to get back. I've got pies to bake tonight and bread to mix for the morning rush."

He nodded and held her hand tight to his. "I won't take you far."

Oh, but he would, she knew. He could, if she let him. Julien was a ladies' man, handsome and playful and larger than life. A man who danced with the girls at the *fais-do-do*. A man who charmed women with just a wink and a smile. He could take her to places she'd stopped dreaming about going. He could also break her heart again.

But Alma had enough heartbreak already to last her a long, long time. She wouldn't add falling for Julien LeBlanc to that list. Not a second time, anyway.

"It is a nice night," she said, just to test her voice to see if she could speak. The sweet scent of honeysuckle tickled her nose.

"It is at that."

He glanced over at her while they strolled along the worn dirt path beside what they called Bayou Petite. It was just a small tributary shooting out of the big open canal that ran along the main road in Fleur. Big Fleur Bayou, that one was called. The town had been built around Big Fleur.

"So you had a productive day?" she asked, simply because being silent made her think way too much about him. And wonder why today of all days, she'd let him get to her.

Maybe because, today of all days, he'd actually made the effort.

"We did. Crawfish season is wide open but prices might be steep. And this year's spring shrimp season has to be better than last fall." He rubbed his hands together. "I'm ready. More than ready."

Alma pushed aside a low cypress branch, the greening of the tree shining in the dusk like fireflies. "It'll soon be time for the spring festival."

"And the blessing of the fleets," Julien added. "We need lots of blessings."

Alma stopped at an old bench. "Let's sit."

Surprised colored his face. "*You* want to sit with *me* a spell, *catin?*"

"I've been on my feet all day." It was the best excuse she could find. She didn't dare tell him that even while making small talk around him, she became breathless.

He gave her a low bow and, with a flourish, wiped the wooden bench clear of fallen leaves and debris. "Your throne awaits, my queen."

Alma laughed at his antics, her face muscles stretching wide. Maybe she should laugh more. "You're such a clown."

He sank down beside her then smiled over at her. "I made you laugh, so I don't mind being called a *couillon*. And you have to know, when you laugh it sounds like a melody."

"You're also full of baloney," she retorted, touched that he liked her laugh. She had to admit, it was good to see him laughing, too. They'd both lost a parent and while her mother had been gone for years, Julien's father had died only a few short months ago. Had that changed Julien?

"I do put on a good show." He went quiet and kept his eyes on her. "But then, you know that better than most."

She couldn't answer that. She did know it better than most. Underneath all that jovial bluster, Julien had a heart as big as the bay. He laughed a lot, talked a lot and held a lot inside.

"It's been a while since we've just sat and visited," he said, looking out at the dark water. "Life just keeps on going."

"It does. I'm always so busy with the café."

"You need to slow down."

"You could take that same advice yourself."

Julien nodded, his actions causing his wild mop of dark hair to fall around his forehead. "Can't rest, darlin'. Too much to do. Work's hard to come by these days."

"You've always been a solid worker."

He turned then, moving close. So close she

could see the flecks of brown in his onyx eyes. "So you have noticed some of my redeeming qualities?"

"You have redeeming qualities?"

He laughed again. "*Non.* Not a one."

But Alma knew that wasn't exactly true. Julien loved living here on this bayou. Like most of the men around here, he'd learned how to fish and hunt while he was still practically in diapers. It was in his blood. And like most of the people she knew, he worked two jobs just to help his family make ends meet. He had changed a lot since high school. She'd heard through the bayou grapevine that he'd stopped drinking after his daddy died.

Alma prayed that was the truth. She prayed that Julien would settle down and find true happiness. But she didn't dare pray that he might one day love her again.

"How's your mama?" she asked now, always worried. The women around here didn't take care of themselves and health care was a joke—not very affordable or available. Julien's mother had a lot of health problems.

"She's doing okay," he said, the sparkle leaving his eyes. "She has her good days. Just has to watch that old ticker. Heart disease ain't pretty."

"Take care of her, Julien."

He took her hand again. "I will, I promise. But what about you and your sisters?"

Alma knew what he was asking. What about the cancer? Are you all safe?

"Callie is doing great. Her last checkup was a positive one—all clear." She thought about what Callie had been through and said a silent prayer for her sister. "And Brenna—you know her. Always going and doing. A busy career woman. But she's good at her job and she loves working for the art gallery. She talks about planning her wedding, but I'm not sure that will ever happen."

He turned toward Alma then. "And you?"

What about her? She couldn't tell him the secrets of her heart. "I'm okay. Tired. Missing my mama today. Wishing for things—"

"What kind of things?"

Alma swallowed back the hopes and dreams, refusing to let them float to the surface. "You know, more money to pay bills and less hours spent in that café. More time with Papa and my sisters. More… I don't know. I'm content, Julien. Just content."

"Is that all you want out of life? To be 'just content'?"

She wanted to shout to him, no, she wanted more. She wanted him to tell her he *had* changed…she wanted to forgive him for his youthful indiscretions. But Alma had been through so much pain, she was almost afraid to look for love and a family. What if she found someone—other than the man staring at her now—and then she got sick like Mama had? Would that person stand by her through such a sickness? Or worse, what if she gave in to Julien's flirtations and fell for him all over again, only to get her heart broken one more time or to only get sick the way her mama had gotten sick? She couldn't put carefree, laid-back Julien through that. She didn't want to put any man through that.

"You have that look, *chère,*" he whispered against her hair.

"What look is that?"

"That faraway look. It breaks my heart."

Did everyone around here know her so well?

"I'll be fine, Julien. It's just, spring always makes me think of Mama. She loved her garden, loved spring on the bayou. It's hard sometimes."

He looked out over the water, his gaze following two fussy wood ducks. "My daddy's birthday is next month."

Alma's heart broke open a little bit. "Oh, that's right. He always loved this time of year. He used to tease that we only had the seafood festival to celebrate his birthday." She touched a hand to Julien's arm. "I miss him, too."

Julien shrugged, as if shaking off the pain. "*Oui,* we all do. But I want to see you laugh again, so let's talk about something else."

She got up, pulling away. "I need to get back."

"But we were just getting started."

Alma looked at her watch. "Your five minutes are up." She turned to head back up the path, this new intimacy startling her and leaving her unsettled. "But I do appreciate the little break."

Julien got up to follow her. "What if I want more than five minutes?"

Shocked, she stopped. "Since when?"

He put his hands on her arms. "Since I'm getting older and wiser and you're getting prettier and smarter." He turned serious then. "I can't seem to settle down, Alma. And I'm thinking it's your fault."

"My fault? You're crazy."

"No, just a man with a purpose. I'm thinking you've spoiled me for other women."

Her pulse jumped like a fish coming out of the water, just a flash. "Then you need to rethink that."

Alma pivoted and started walking. She heard him running to catch up with her. What had come over him?

His words echoed up to her. "You like bothering me, don't you? I mean, you like making me suffer."

"I don't want to be a bother," she said over her shoulder. "And I don't have time to make anyone suffer."

Except herself.

"You are a bother, though. You won't go away. Always in my head, always the smell of flowers and the image of those pretty eyes of yours."

There went her pulse, her heart, again. "I don't want to be there—inside your head. Let me out."

He tugged her back just as they reached the back porch of the café. "I can't shake you."

"So what are you going to do about it, Julien?"

He didn't speak. But he did something, all right.

He leaned down and kissed her smack on the lips. A long, measured, meandering kiss that bubbled and churned with as many undercurrents as that big bayou. His kiss was certainly as dangerous as those ancient waters.

She pulled away long enough to whisper a plea. "Stop it, Julien."

But he didn't stop, even when the few customers and workers on the big porch started whistling and clapping.

Chapter Three

"How did you hear that?"

Alma glared at her cell phone then put it back to her ear.

Her sister Brenna laughed, the sound tinkling like chimes through the phone line. "Are you kidding? I still have friends in Fleur, you know. Friends with cell phones and social networks. They keep me informed. I even have a picture. Hold on."

Alma groaned then glanced out the window of the cottage where she lived behind the restaurant. Less than two hours since Julien had pulled that stunt and already it had gone viral.

Her sister's silky voice returned. "Okay. I sent you a copy. Look."

"I don't have time—" But she looked anyway. "Oh, wow."

"Oh, wow is right," Brenna said, giggling again. "That would look good on a romance novel cover."

"Yeah, right. Don't get any ideas."

"Oh, I only have one idea," Brenna said with a sigh. "We need a wedding in Fleur. And you and Julien have been dancing around this thing since high school. Actually, since kindergarten."

"We're not dancing around," Alma retorted. "We're just friends."

"Friends? Sister, that shot shows you and Julien LeBlanc are so much more than friends."

"Delete it," Alma said. "That's what I'm going to do right now."

"No, you won't," Brenna said. "You'll print it out and put it in that scrapbook you've been working on for years."

"And how do you know about my scrapbook?"

"I have ways."

"You are so sneaky. No wonder you're good at your job."

"And what does that mean?"

"Nothing," Alma said. "Just that your imagination makes you suspect things and I guess that is a bit creative when you're dealing with art. You can spot a fake."

"Exactly," Brenna said. "Julien tries to be a fake, pretending to be a bad boy and all that, but he's still in love with you. That's why he pretends to leave a trail of broken hearts behind him. But he's the one with the broken heart. And now I have the picture to prove it. You know what they say about a picture?"

"Well, this one isn't speaking a thousand words," Alma replied. "More like, this picture is purely, truly fake." She swallowed, then closed her eyes to the memory of Julien's kiss. It had not felt as if he were faking at all. No, that kiss had been all too real. "He only did that to embarrass me and get me all riled up."

"Okay, keep telling yourself that," Brenna said. "I think you are riled up, but in a good way."

"And what about you?" Alma asked, anxious to get off the subject of that kiss and the way it had made her feel. "When are you going to have that big Baton Rouge wedding you keep dreaming about?"

Her sister went silent. And that wasn't like Brenna.

"Bree?"

"Not a good subject right now." Alma heard a sigh. "Keep the picture, Alma. You'll regret it if you delete it. I gotta go. Hope to see you in a few weeks."

The connection ended and Alma was left standing there, staring at a picture of Julien LeBlanc kissing her.

"I should delete it," she said, mumbling and muttering as she went around locking doors and preparing to go to bed.

But she didn't.

She got in her grandmother's old brass bed laced with mosquito netting and stared at the picture for a long time.

Then she turned out the lights and tried to go to sleep.

But the face of a dark-haired charmer kept popping into her mind. And the memory of that kiss kept her tossing and turning well into the wee hours.

Why did Julien want to be back in her life?

Julien wasn't the first one in the door at the Fleur Bakery and Café the next morning. He waited until almost lunchtime, not wanting to appear anxious.

Except that he couldn't wait to see Alma again. She'd kissed him back last night, and for the first time in a long time he had real hope in his heart. Since the night she'd walked out of his life, Julien had longed for a way to win Alma back. But pride and her aloof nature had held him back.

Then Sunday after church, he'd watched his *maman* with his cousin's new baby. Watched and seen the tears forming in his sweet mother's eyes. She missed her husband. Julien's daddy had died from a heart attack just last fall. They all missed him. When his mother Virginia had glanced up and caught him staring at her and the child, she'd said something that had stayed with Julien.

"Don't squander time with your pride, Julien. You don't have to look so sad. You could have a baby yourself if you stop being so mule-headed. Alma would make a good mother."

His mama sure had a way with words. But her pointed suggestion had stayed with Julien and then he'd spotted Alma the very next day there in her café, with that early morning sweetness all around her. He'd seen the same sadness he felt there in her pretty eyes. She'd looked as if she wanted something more. Something she couldn't quite find.

That's how he felt now.

He wanted her to smile again. Preferably, at him. And the fact that she'd kissed him back rather than slapping him flat gave him enough hope to hang on like a bass on a nylon string.

Time to let her reel him in.

Enough with the revelations and the signs. He planned to ask Alma out on a real date. If he could get up the courage. Maybe a poem. He'd quote her some pretty lines then ask her to go to up to New Orleans for a nice evening. Alma deserved a nice evening, didn't she?

After a few of his fishing buddies converged on the restaurant, Julien made his way to his favorite table then searched for Alma. Where was she?

Another waitress came and took his order, her own soft smile full of interest. Mollie, her name tag stated. But instead of flirting in his usual way, Julien only had an interest in the chief cook and bottle washer around here. Alma. It wasn't like her to take time away from the café.

Maybe she was hiding out. He'd thought about not showing up today himself. She had not been happy with him after that kiss.

He grinned, remembering how she'd turned and pranced back into the restaurant, all fire and glory, while everyone who'd witnessed the event had clapped and whooped.

Alma wasn't into clapping and whooping.

Julien had walked home, whistling a happy tune.

Until reality set in and he realized he'd kissed Alma in public. And while she'd acted like she liked it, she'd also acted like she just maybe might kill him. Later. She probably thought he'd done it on purpose, just to show her. On purpose, to send her a message that Julien LeBlanc still had it.

Whatever "it" was. Lately, it hadn't been working for him. So he'd reached out to the one woman who could always make him smile even when his heart carried a big frown. So he'd kissed that woman in a moment of pure, spontaneous need.

What if she poisoned his food?

"You look like a nutria caught in a trap," Tebow said as he slid into the booth across from Julien. "What's on your mind, bro?"

The cute waitress dropped Julien's plate of eggs and grits in front of him then took Tebow's order. "Bon appetit," she said, winking at Julien.

Julien glanced over at his friend. "Here, take a bite of these eggs."

Tebow shrugged and dug right in. "They're good."

Julien watched his friend for any sign of distress then pulled his plate back.

"Hey!"

"Get your own," he told Tebow, still looking around for Alma.

When the girl named Mollie returned to give Julien a refill on his coffee, he asked her, "Where's Alma today?"

Looking surprised, the waitress held the glass coffeepot close. "She had a meeting about the festival. She'll be in later."

Tebow shot the waitress a big smile then aimed his baby-blue gaze at the nametag on the girl's T-shirt. "Thank you, Pretty Mollie."

Mollie gave him a look that told him to drop dead then whirled and headed away.

"I think you just broke her heart," he said

to Julien. "And I think she just broke my heart in return."

"What?" Julien asked between bites. He needed to hurry.

"Never mind." Tebow stared longingly at the food. "I'll just sit here and watch you eat while I starve to death from lack of love and a meal."

"Where's the festival committee meeting?" Julien asked.

Tebow shrugged. "You're asking me?"

"Yes, you. You mama is always on that committee."

"And they always meet at the family center at the church," Tebow said, giving Julien a strange look. "I'm worried about you, bro."

Julien shoved the rest of his grits into his mouth, swallowed and then took a long swig of coffee. "I have to go."

Slapping a ten on the table, he was up and out the door before Tebow could ask why and what for.

Julien had come to a decision after that kiss last night. He was tired of waiting around for Alma to forgive him. He'd just have to show her he could change—he had changed—instead of hoping she'd see it with her own eyes.

He was about to volunteer to serve on the Fleur Seafood Festival Committee.

He loved a good festival and he loved seafood.

And he wanted to kiss Alma again. Soon.

If he had to sit around in boring meetings to make that happen, it would be a small sacrifice.

Alma stifled a yawn and looked at her watch. She was cranky today and it didn't help that she'd missed part of her eight hours of sleep. But the breakfast shift would be changing over to lunch and she needed to get back to the café.

Tebow's formidable mama, Frances LaBorde, was chattering away about what they could do to bring new and exciting ideas to the annual seafood festival scheduled for next month.

"We have all the usual sponsors lined up and we're right on schedule as far as food booths and entertainment," Mrs. LaBorde said. "Alma, you got the seafood wagons all ready?"

Alma sat up straight and picked up her pen. "Yes, ma'am. The Fleur Bakery and Café will have booths stationed at both entries to the festival. And of course, we'll have a booth and cooker set up right in front of the café, too. Crawfish, shrimp and oysters, fried and boiled, and just about any type of fresh fish you could ask for. Not to mention boudin, gumbo, dirty rice and red beans and rice. No one will go hungry."

Alma's robust daddy, Ramon, winked at her

then turned to the woman who'd asked Alma the question. "Now, Frances, you know my girl's gonna do it up right, just as she always does. Alma hires extra help for the festival."

Frances, a plump widow who had an extreme crush on Alma's papa, beamed a smile at Ramon. "*Oui,* our Alma always does a fine job with the food." Then Frances gave Ramon another smile. "And I imagine you'll have your boat ready for tours and fishing trips?"

"Same as always," Ramon said, lifting his dark eyebrows. Ramon Blanchard's jolly expression changed to one of insult and injury. "Do you doubt me, Frances?"

"No, never, Ramon. You're as dependable as the tide. I know you'll entertain the tourists with your boat tours."

Alma had to hide her grin. Her papa looked about as aggravated as she felt. Usually, she got all excited about the seafood festival, but today… she had other things on her mind.

The door to the fellowship hall swung open and the very main thing she had on her mind walked in.

Julien LeBlanc in the flesh.

And looking too good in that flesh.

Everyone looked at Julien then at Alma.

Alma looked at Julien then looked at her daddy.

Her daddy glowered at her then glowered at Julien.

This was awkward. She thought of that kiss and felt a flush moving up her neck.

"Can we help you, Julien?" Mrs. LaBorde asked with a sweet smile plastered on her pink lips.

Julien walked up with his hands held together. "I came to help you, Miss Frances. I want to volunteer—for the committee. To help in any way I can."

Alma slid low in her chair. Why, oh, why was he here? Julien didn't like being stuck inside four walls. He liked being outside with the wind in his face and some sort of pole or trap in his hand. He liked the swamp, loved water more than land, trees more than paper.

And he surely didn't like committee work.

Frances LaBorde seemed at a loss for words, a first for her.

Papa grunted and went into a long statement, all in Cajun French. Alma heard enough of it to know her daddy wasn't pleased with Julien's antics. He'd already read her the riot act over that public display of affection, telling her he'd had to hear it from the mailman and the preacher. News always traveled with lightning speed in Fleur.

He'd told her, "I don't trust him, Alma. Not one little bit."

Her papa had never trusted Julien. Maybe she should remember that.

Both the mayor and the minister chimed in on Julien's sudden civic responsibility.

"That's wonderful, Julien," Mayor Daigle said, his almost bald head bobbing like a cork. "We need some fresh ideas in this discussion."

He got a frown from Frances and a smile from Julien.

Reverend Guidry offered Julien a seat.

Right by Alma.

"C'mon in and sit down," he said to Julien, obviously oblivious to the undercurrents in the room. "New members are always needed."

"Thank you, Reverend," Julien said, winking over at Alma. He dropped like a catfish right into his chair. "Hello, Alma."

"Hi," she said, her voice just below a squeak. Then she shot him a look that could fry fish. Especially catfish.

Julien just kept on smiling. "Now, don't let me interrupt. Alma can bring me up-to-date later."

The way he said that made Alma want to spit nails, even while his smooth voice poured over her like warm butter. But her papa's frowning face made her sit up and look stern. So she went over her notes to hide her mortification.

Frances finally closed her mouth and started

talking again. "Well, uh, where were we? Oh, yes. Cotton candy. Who's in charge of cotton candy?"

Julien leaned close to Alma. "You are as sweet as cotton candy."

"Shh," she said in a hiss of breath.

"Would you like to be in charge, Julien?" Frances asked, clearly upset that he was making mischief while she had the floor. "We need someone to organize cotton candy, popcorn and funnel cakes."

Julien gave Alma another breathtaking smile. "I'd be glad to handle that, Miss Frances. What do I need to do?"

Reverend Guidry raised a hand. "We have all the equipment at the church. Just line up your volunteers and we can order the needed supplies. All the proceeds from those endeavors go back to the church for the youth fund."

Alma finally found her voice. "You can get some of the youth to help you with manning the booths. But remind them the festival starts early and lasts until well into the night. They can't leave their booths during their assigned times to work."

"That sounds easy enough," Julien said, tapping his fingers on the table. "Youths to work. Long hours. Order supplies. Got it."

"You might want to take notes," Frances suggested.

Papa frowned. "Are you sure you can handle

this, Julien? You know how young people can be so wishy-washy."

"Got it," Julien replied, holding a finger to his temple, his confidence overwhelming in the face of Ramon Blanchard's scorn and doubt. "I have a very good memory." He gave Alma a long, appraising glance when he said that.

Alma heard her papa's huff of disgust then endured another warm blush. She was going to strangle Julien LeBlanc. She didn't know why he'd suddenly decided to become her shadow. But she did know she needed to stop him right now.

After a few more uncomfortable minutes, Frances called the meeting adjourned. Alma got up and grabbed her papers and her purse to make a beeline for the door.

"Hey, wait up," Julien called, catching up with her, his hand on the door so she could pass. Or not pass.

"I have to get back to the café," she said, not daring to stop and let him have it right here with such a captivated audience hanging on their every word.

"I'll walk you, then."

"I know the way."

"Of course you know the way. But I'd still like to escort you, as a courtesy."

Alma waited until they'd made it past the

church parking lot, then she stopped and turned to him. "What do you think you're doing, Julien?"

He looked around then pointed a finger to his chest. "Me? I'm walking you to work. Kind of romantic, don't you think?"

"Why aren't you at work?"

"I was, before the sun came up. I stopped in to have a late breakfast and you…were missing."

"So you tracked me down and embarrassed me yet again?"

She started up, trotting off at a fast pace, but felt his hand warm on her arm. "I don't want to embarrass you, *catin*."

"Then what do you call this?"

Julien leaned close, his dark eyes holding hers. "I call this making up for lost time. I'm yours, Alma. And I believe it's time we both get used to that idea."

Alma's shock caused her to gasp. "Mine? You were never mine. And I'll never be yours. You might have considered that before you decided to launch an attack on me."

"I'm not attacking, darlin'," he said on a sultry whisper. "I'm wooing. Yes, that's what I'm doing. I want to make you mine."

"Well, good luck with that." She pulled away and started toward the café, her heartbeat pounding right along with her espadrilles.

She refused to even hope that Julien LeBlanc

might actually be serious. How many times had she seen him sweet-talking other women? Too many to count. She might have fallen for that ploy in high school, but she was a grown woman now.

And she had two very good reasons to keep her distance from Julien. One, he'd broken her heart. And two, she carried a high risk of getting a disease that could kill her the way it had killed her mother and destroyed her sister's life. Breast cancer wasn't pretty. The odds didn't look good. And the odds of Julien being able to deal with breast cancer didn't look good either.

"Stop this nonsense," she said, even while, in her battered heart, hope bloomed as brightly as Callie's flowers.

"I'm just getting started, Alma," Julien called after her.

"I mean it."

Alma kept on walking. But her heart shouted loud and clear in its bumpy little chamber. And its plea echoed inside her head until she'd made it into the café and shut the door.

Prove it, Julien. Please prove it.

Chapter Four

He set out to prove himself to Alma.

He began with flowers, straight from her sister's sweet nursery. The Blanchard girls loved flowers.

"What do you suggest?" Julien asked Callie two days later, after he'd tried talking to Alma.

Too busy to talk, that one.

But not too busy to stop and smell the roses.

"For Alma?" Callie shot him a level look, as if she might be comparing him to a bug on a leaf. "Why? Did somebody die? Or did you make her mad again?"

"She's always mad and no, nobody died. I just want to send her some flowers is all."

Callie smiled, but her sparkling eyes held a hint of doubt. "Hmm. She'll be even madder now—mostly with me if I sell you an arrangement."

"Do you want my business or not?" Julien

asked, figuring like everyone around here, Callie couldn't afford to turn him away.

"I do need business. It's a slow morning." She shook her head when he touched a finger to some fat red roses. "You don't want to send her those. Too predictable for my sister."

Frustration singed through him. "Then what do I need to send?"

"She has a thing for Louisiana irises. Alma likes things that just kind of spring up." The look Callie gave him indicated he might be the exception to that.

"Then irises it is," Julien replied, thinking, in spite of Callie's questioning look, that he could spring up right along with the plants.

"I have a pretty one just about to bud in a nice pot," Callie said. "She can put it on the front porch for now and then plant it later, maybe in Grand-mère's backyard."

"Why does she live in that old cottage anyway?" Julien asked, wondering why Alma didn't live with their father in the big house on the edge of town where she'd grown up. The tiny little house tipped toward the bayou was quaint and pretty but a bit run-down and old.

Callie gave him another scrutinizing look then shrugged. "It's near the restaurant and it keeps her close to our grandmother. Alma and Grand-mère were close. We are all close."

She went to the rear of the big open floral shop and brought back a brightly painted pot holding one fat bulb with rich green shoots poking out of the moist, dark dirt. "Besides, why do you care all of a sudden?"

The Blanchard sisters were direct and they stuck together like a flock of geese. Could get just as mad as a fighting goose, too. He'd need to remember that.

"I don't know," he said, opting for honesty. Because even though his heart was tugging toward Alma and all that entailed, he wasn't so sure of himself regarding how to go about achieving that particular goal. This turnaround was recent and still a bit shaky. He was still adrift but trying to find his way. "I guess…I just think it's time."

"Well, amen to that," Callie said, giving him a card to go with the iris. "Do you want to write something? And are you going to deliver this, or should I?"

"I want you to deliver it," he said, squinting while he tried to recall a verse. "I want her to be surprised. I'll check in with her later."

"This might get interesting," Callie said. Then she leaned across the counter. "Just don't hurt her, Julien. That wouldn't be good."

She gave him a lift of her arched brows to back up that statement.

"I don't plan on hurting her. Not anymore."

He paid Callie and stood there, staring at the little square of creamy paper, while Callie waited on another customer.

Then he grinned and wrote what he wanted to say. In big, bold, black letters.

"Je voudrais sortir avec toi."

The card read "I would like to go out with you."

Alma said it out loud again in French, the words playing a pretty tune off her tongue.

She stared at the single iris, knowing it would bloom a beautiful violet-blue one day.

Winnie came to stand beside her and both women stared at the blue and green-colored pot sitting on the counter.

Winnie read the card. "He wants to take you out on a date."

"I get that," Alma said, shaking her head. "What are we, fifteen again?"

"Maybe he wants things to be the way they were when you were fifteen."

"Things can never be that way again," Alma said, her eyes still on the bulb. The tender shoots of green were piercing the earth, breaking through to grow and form a beautiful flower.

One of her favorites. Maybe because she'd had to do the same, pierce through and grow up. Too quickly. Maybe she was just a late bloomer in the love department.

Or maybe she was too afraid to let go and go out on a real date with Julien. If she did that, she'd be crossing a line they'd long ago drawn in the sand. She'd always been caught between her feelings for Julien and her need to spread her wings and fly out of the nest. Her *former* feelings for Julien, she thought, correcting herself. And, maybe, her former need to fly away. Her life had become so routine, Alma wasn't sure she could change it now.

But flowers. And not just any flowers. A bulb that, once planted, would take root and spread across her garden to bloom for years to come. Was Julien sending her a message?

She had a sick feeling that her sister had betrayed her by working with the enemy. But was Julien her enemy? Or was he trying to make amends after all this time. But why now?

"Are you gonna plant it?" Winnie asked, her smile as knowing as a cat's. "Or let it die a slow death in that pot?"

"I haven't decided yet."

Alma took the iris and set it away from the cash register. She'd display it for all to see and then she'd decide what to do about the flower. And about Julien's request.

He was waiting for her after work.
"Hello."

Alma looked down at him, taking in the way he hovered there on the bottom step. "How long have you been out here?"

"Not long. Just got here. And right on time."

Not used to having him around so much, Alma glanced behind her to make sure everyone had left. Then she turned and hurried down the steps. "It's late, Julien. Go home and get some rest."

He gave her a look similar to the one he'd had right before he'd kissed her. "I'm not tired."

"Well, I am."

He fell in beside her as she walked the short distance to the little white cottage sitting like a dollhouse underneath an ancient cypress tree. The house was precariously close to the dark waters of the bayou. Alma often spotted alligators and snakes in the water just a few feet from her back dock. But tonight she feared the most dangerous predator was walking on two feet beside her.

"I'll make you a nice cup of herbal tea," he said, not skipping a beat. "And my mama made tea cakes this afternoon." He pulled a bag around. "Fresh outta the oven."

Alma loved Mrs. LeBlanc's tea cakes.

"We used to eat those after school," she said before she could catch herself.

"*Oui,* that we did. It'll be like old times."

His triumphant tone nettled at her like a thorny bush. Grabbing the bag, she turned at the door.

"But we've both changed since then, haven't we? I have to go."

"Alma?"

"Thank you, Julien. For the iris and for the tea cakes. I can make my own tea. Good night."

Alma closed the door and bolted it both against her racing heart and Julien's crestfallen expression.

That had not gone the way he'd planned.

Julien stood there, his hands on his hips, the scent of her soap-clean lotion still swirling around his nose.

The iris should have done it. The tea cakes should have sealed the deal. She was obviously playing hard to get. He'd just have to keep trying.

He was about to call it a night when he heard the cottage door opening back up. Alma poked her head out. "I just have one question," she said, looking down at her feet. "Why are you doing this now? Why now after all these years?"

He didn't dare make a move toward her. Putting his hands in the pocket of his old cargo pants, he stared up at her and said, "I don't know. Except lately, I've felt this tugging in my heart and when I saw you standing all alone in the café the other morning, something changed inside me. You looked so alone, so sad."

He shrugged, stared off into the night, the

sounds of the bayou singing all around him. Then he managed to spill his guts. "Your parents had a special kind of thing and I know you miss your mama. We all miss her. And I miss my daddy and his birthday is coming up and so I can get how you have bad days sometimes. I guess I just want to make you smile again, Alma. Really smile. The way you used to smile."

She opened the door and came out onto the porch, but she wasn't smiling at all. "So you think flowers and cookies will do the trick?"

He advanced a couple of inches. "I think you like flowers and cookies. Or at least you used to."

"I used to like a lot of things."

With that, she turned to go back inside.

"Alma, why don't you sit here with me?"

She turned at the door, her blue eyes inky in the muted moonlight. "I'll be all right, Julien. I don't know if I'll ever be the same after losing my mama and watching Callie suffer. I'm afraid of what might lay ahead for me."

He stepped up onto the porch. *"C'est pour toi que je suis.* I'm here for you, Alma. No matter what. You have to know that."

She moved toward him and Julien's heart leapt with joy.

Alma put a hand on his face, her touch like a warm breeze, feather-light and tingling. "I can't be sure of that, now, can I? And that's the problem here, now, with you deciding out of the blue you want to woo me. You've had a long time to reach this decision. And I've been waiting all that time. It won't hurt to wait a little longer. It won't hurt to be very sure."

Then she pulled her hand away and went to the door.

She was gone before Julien could catch his breath. But he could still see her eyes there in the moonlight.

Her beautiful, doubting eyes.

Alma put the cookies on the counter and stared at the bag.

Her heart wanted her to open that door and let Julien in.

Her head told her to bar the door and run for cover.

It wasn't just that he'd hurt her so badly on what should have been one of the best nights of her life. Boys kissed other girls all the time. And half the time, they didn't mean to do it. And the other half of the time, they meant to do it but never meant to make good on it. But that night, her Julien had been so angry and so reckless when he'd stomped off the dance floor and proceeded to humiliate her. He'd drunk some spiked punch, a lot of spiked punch. Then he'd danced with other girls and he'd wound up kissing another girl. Without regard for Alma and her feelings.

That was the part that hurt the most.

But there had been more than the problem of Julien drinking too much and Alma picking a fight with him because of it. And there had been more than him turning to the first pretty girl who passed by to make a bold point with Alma. Julien had always worried that she would go away and never come back. They'd argued about *that* on their special night.

And in his worries, he'd caused that very thing to happen. But she hadn't gone away, she'd just stepped out of his arms.

Alma had big dreams, but she'd always thought she'd have Julien to share those dreams. She believed she could go and do and come home and he'd be here, waiting. Or even better, he'd travel with her and see the world she so often talked about.

Julien wasn't going anywhere. And therein lay the main problem still simmering between them. Julien loved Fleur, Louisiana, more than he could ever love her. And she cared about him too much to ask him to leave with her. It wouldn't be right. He'd be miserable. And that would make her miserable, too.

So if he was waiting for her, he might have

to keep waiting. Alma was just marking time until…

She stopped, stilled. Until what? Until her daddy wasn't grieving so much? Until her sister Callie was married and happy and chasing children around the flower gardens? Until Brenna finally married her long-time boyfriend and settled into the life she loved in Baton Rouge?

Or was Alma waiting for the day when she truly knew Julien loved her enough to let her go?

Julien might pretend to be a man about town, but Alma had always suspected he hid a lot of angst underneath those killer smiles. And, she reminded herself with a spark of hope, he'd never brought another woman into the café.

Not once in all these years.

Julien should have moved on by now. Alma had suffered through watching him with other women, but she'd also rejoiced when he'd broken things off with those other women. Alma shouldn't hold it against him if he did fall for someone else since she'd dated other people now and again. Those men didn't make her feel the way Julien could make her feel—alive, all warm and fuzzy, full of excitement and anticipation. They didn't have staying power. And since her mother's sickness and death, she'd rarely had a date. Now she wasn't so sure *she* had staying power.

It hurt too much to think about what might

happen down the road. It hurt too much to think about what she'd had and lost.

And tonight, it still hurt too much to let go and give in to Julien's sudden change of heart. Because he loved his life here and she wanted a life out there. And because she might not have much time to explore the world or…love a man. Her mother had run out of time and Callie had lost her husband and now had too much time on her hands. Brenna didn't have enough time in each day even to plan her wedding.

But what if Alma could make it work? What if Julien was the kind of man who was willing to truly love her, no matter what? He'd have to prove it to her. He'd have to make her see that he was willing to settle down and grow up and…be there.

Just be there. No matter what.

Alma wouldn't open up her heart to that kind of commitment unless it was solid.

So she put on her pajamas and took the ancient enamel tea kettle and made herself a cup of peppermint tea. Then she opened the crumbled bag Julien had shoved at her and took out a fat, buttery, yellow tea cake. She nibbled it while she stared out into the moonlight and remembered how, long ago, Julien and she would sit and eat tea cakes, their feet dangling in the bayou water, their eyes on each other. He'd kiss her, the taste

of vanilla and butter all around them. And they'd
laugh and whisper and dream of the future they'd
have together.

The future that had disappeared in the swirling wisps of satin and lace as Alma had turned
and run away from him. Had she been running
away from the constraints of a life on the bayou?
Or had she believed she was running toward free-
dom?

No, her heart hurt too much to ever enjoy free-
dom. Her guilt at even wanting to break away
from her hometown shadowed her like Spanish
moss. Sometimes she felt trapped and sometimes
she felt captivated.

"I don't know if I can ever leave," she said into
the night. Then she stood and remembered and
closed her eyes to all the wants in her life. And
reminded herself of her blessings and of all the
things she couldn't have.

Never knowing that the man she was thinking about was still standing out there under the
cypress tree, wondering how to win her back.

Chapter Five

Julien couldn't look away. He couldn't move from the spot under the big towering cypress tree. How could his life have changed so completely in the blink of an eye? Yes, it had to do with seeing Alma all sad and lonely the other day in the early morning light. It also had to do with knowing she'd suffered through such a tragedy that she could barely function. But he saw that in spite of her difficulties, she did indeed make it through her days with a sweet grace and a strong sense of faith. That didn't make sense since he'd been hovering around during her mother's death and her older sister's cancer scare. He'd often asked after each of them, yet hadn't taken things any further than comfort and platitudes with Alma during all of that. He'd been too afraid to push at her fragile, tattered emotions. And he respected her and her family way too much to make any moves during the worst of their grief.

But oh, how he'd longed to hold her in his arms and comfort her. He still wanted to do that.

Why now? Why did he have to stand here pining away for a woman who had long ago given up on him? Pining now, when all these years past he'd accepted that he'd lost her forever.

Julien thought back over the day last week when he'd had the first of his epiphanies. He'd been at his boat warehouse, working on a sweet pirogue that he hoped to finish and sell at the upcoming festival. The small city park was right across from the old warehouse. He'd heard children playing. He'd watched their laughter and their tears, watched young mothers soothing hurt feelings and opening juice containers and doling out crackers. And he'd wanted that for himself. With Alma.

He'd gone home that day with her on his mind. And that night, he'd lain in bed and said a prayer for the good Lord to offer him some sort of validation. He'd waffled back and forth for years now, playing the field while he hoped Alma would turn back to him. Was it time to try and win Alma back?

Then he'd seen his mama holding a baby. His cousin's first child and, again, that longing had hit him. The next morning as he was leaving the house, his mama had stopped her knitting to stare up at him.

"I want grandchildren before I pass, Julien. I can't have that if you don't settle down and get married. *Va chercher ton vrai amour bientôt.* Go after her."

Find your true love soon. Go after Alma?

Another sign? Or just his *maman* complaining?

Except his tired, fragile mama never complained. Never.

Julien had it in his head that if his mama passed without knowing he was happily settled, he'd never forgive himself. He'd already let down his poor papa. That hard-working man had died way too young and knowing both of his sons were still playing the field and fooling around with life.

Was Julien rushing into something just to appease his widowed mother? Or was his widowed mother pushing him toward the thing he wanted most in the whole world?

Alma Blanchard.

Why had he waited so long to make this woman his own? Was it because spring was blooming in all its glory and children were springing up in the park like spider lilies? Was it because he was growing up and getting older and wiser? Or was it truly just because his poor dear mother was sick and weary and a widow and he hated seeing her like that?

All of the above and more.

His mama's sweet, calculated suggestion had come exactly when he'd needed to hear it. And then when he was already feeling down because of his deceased daddy's upcoming birthday, he'd seen Alma standing there all alone in that quaint little café, like some maiden from long ago waiting for her lost love.

Was it fate that Julien had been standing at the door, waiting for her to let him in? Or was it faith?

His poet's heart told him it was both.

"*Oui,* I hear you, Lord."

Julien wasn't a faithful churchgoer, but he had an ongoing conversation with God since he was alone a lot, surrounded by the primitive beauty of the swamp, and he figured it couldn't hurt to keep God close.

Now, right now, when he glanced up at that dollhouse of a cottage and thought about the sweet doll living there, Julien felt the breath of the Lord rushing over him right along with the sweet-scented breeze coming off the bayou. Should he pray? Or should he go home?

Julien started walking, deciding he could most certainly walk and pray at the same time.

His phone buzzed inside his shirt pocket.

Hoping it would be Alma, ready to invite him inside, he frowned.

It wasn't Alma.

"Oui?"

"Bro, where are you?"

"Pierre, where do you think I am?" His little brother was such a worrier.

"Me, I don't know. Thought we were meeting up at the Backwater."

Julien hit a hand on his forehead. "I forgot. I'm on my way."

He'd planned to meet Pierre, all right. Right after he'd sweet-talked Alma a little bit. Since the sweet-talking hadn't gone so great, he'd stayed by that tree, stewing in his disappointment instead of heading out to the dump-of-an-oyster bar on the edge of town to have a little sit-down talk with his wild brother.

Pierre was teetering on a narrow path. He could go one way or the other—and right now Julien was the only thing standing between Pierre and a bad, bad future.

Another reason Virginia LeBlanc was sad these days. Julien wouldn't let his mama suffer worrying about her baby boy. He'd just have to explain to Pierre that he was too young and too stupid to keep doing the things he'd been doing.

So it was off to the Backwater.

The burden of being the man of the family

weighed heavily on Julien tonight. His daddy had been a strong, stoic man who'd worked too hard and died too fast from a massive heart attack.

Julien stopped, realizing why his mother's suggestion to him just a few days ago had gotten to him so much.

He didn't want to drop dead somewhere out in the swamp, alone and unloved. And that could very well happen if he didn't convince Alma to forgive him and marry him. Because if he couldn't have Alma, he didn't want all the rest. No other woman would do. He'd rather die alone than die without Alma. Only he didn't want to die without Alma.

If he behaved and played his cards right, he could live a long and wonderful life with Alma before he went to meet his maker.

And maybe they'd have a passel of laughing, dancing children who'd play in the park.

But first, he had to straighten out his little brother.

Even though the prime oyster season had ended a couple of months ago, the Backwater was still hopping with customers. That might be because of the liquid refreshment rather than the food. Julien didn't indulge in heavy drinking anymore. He'd sobered up real quick last fall after his father died, but he should have learned his lesson the night of the senior prom. The night he'd lost Alma. It had taken him too long to finally realize he had to make a change for the better.

But his little brother, twenty-one but going on I-know-everything-so-leave-me-alone, had yet to understand the consequences of his actions. Pierre thought he could handle drinking and making sense at the same time. Julien had been called to one too many dives in the middle of the night to believe his off-kilter younger sibling had a handle on real life. Pierre seemed to think he could party the night away and still get through his daylight time just fine, thank you.

Julien had seen otherwise. If Pierre kept showing up late and missing work, his days as a welder in the nearby shipyard would soon be over.

He aimed to have yet another talk with Pierre.

Pulling his pickup close to the tilted cedar-and-tin building that hung at a jaunty angle over the Intracoastal Waterway like a work cap slung over a stevedore's head, Julien searched the parking lot for his brother's motorcycle. Sure enough, the shiny chrome-and-black beauty was parked off to the side of the building.

Pierre had a steady job working as an equipment repairman on boats and ships, but he shouldn't be overspending on fancy toys. The kid was just barely making the payments on the bike.

Julien shook his head, glancing back at the late

model pickup that he'd inherited after his father died. It got him to and fro. He didn't want for much. His little brother had grand ideas and a not-so-grand way of making those ideas come to fruition.

He found Pierre at the bar, nuzzling up to a pretty, dark-haired girl in tight jeans and an even tighter T-shirt.

Last year, Julien might have been doing the same.

This time, he only thought of Alma.

He didn't know whether to rejoice or recoil.

"Hey, there you are," Pierre called, his words slurred, his eyes wild. "C'mon, bro, have a drink with us."

He tugged Julien close. "This is Rogenna. Pretty Rogenna. My new friend for the evening... and maybe beyond."

Julien smiled at the starry-eyed young woman then turned to glare at his brother. "A word, Pierre?"

"Okay. What word would you like?"

A few choice ones came to mind. Giving Rogenna another smile, Julien grabbed his brother by the collar and pushed him toward the front of the restaurant.

Pierre tried to twist away. "Hey, I wasn't done with my beer."

"I think you are done," Julien said, nodding

to those he recognized, his embarrassment concealed behind a winning grin. "You promised me you'd be sober so we could talk like two adults."

"That's the problem," Pierre said on a loud whine. "You don't think I'm an adult. You and Ma—"

"Do not disrespect our mother," Julien warned, his grin gone now that he had his brother outside and up against the weathered cedar wall. "Why did you go and get drunk again after I warned you last weekend?"

"I was thirsty," Pierre said, an exaggerated smile making him look young and carefree.

Julien ignored the strong smell of beer wafting out in the air but held Pierre pinned to the building. "You can't keep doing this. It can only lead to trouble."

"Says you."

"Yes, says me. Do you want Maman to find you this way?"

"She'll be asleep by the time I get home." Pierre moved to go back inside, but Julien pushed him again.

"I'm not finished," he told his brother. "You need to sober up so we can have a civilized conversation."

Pierre's frown crinkled his face in half. "Don't need to talk to you. You're not my daddy."

Julien heard the hurt behind that remark. And

felt it deep in his bones. "No, I'm not. No one can ever replace Papa. But I can tell you that you are going to regret this lifestyle if you don't slow down."

Pierre stared out into the night, anger warring with regret in his eyes. "Just having fun the way you *used to.*"

"Fun is good, no doubt about that," Julien said, remembering his own wild days. "But too much fun can turn into a bad thing. You could lose your job, or worse, get hurt. You don't need to be driving that bike if you're drunk, P-boy."

Pierre glanced at his bike with a lopsided grin. "I can handle it, bro."

"Are you sure?" Julien let him go and backed up. "Show me. Can you walk a straight line?"

Pierre snorted out a laugh. "Course I can." He proceeded to show Julien just how steady and stable he was.

And wobbled like a floating cork on a choppy sea over the shell-scattered parking lot.

"Yeah, right," Julien said, grabbing his brother again. "Let's go."

"No." Pierre pulled away. "I'm not ready to go."

"You can't drive yourself," Julien argued, hoping he wouldn't have to get physical with his only sibling.

"Yes, I can. I'll be okay in a few minutes."

"I can't risk that." Julien looked at the bike then

back to his brother. "We'll leave your bike here and I'll drive you home."

"Might get stolen."

"I'll make sure Miss Maggie and her sons know you're leaving it here."

Maggie Sonnier had raised three boys of her own and now they all worked for her. The woman would understand Julien's concerns and she'd make sure Pierre's fancy bike was safe.

"What about Rogenna?" Pierre said, glancing back through the screen door where the jukebox and the pretty girl beckoned him. "She owes me another dance."

"Rogenna will be just fine," Julien replied, thinking this right here was part of the reason he had to straighten up his own act. He had to be a better example to his little brother.

Because he wanted his mother to have grand-children from *both* of her sons. In order to make that happen, he needed to make sure Pierre quit partying so much. Not sure how to do that, he slapped his dazed brother on the back and tugged him forward.

"Time to go home and go to sleep."

Pierre squinted at his watch. "It's early. Let's go to Skeeter's house."

"Oh, no. We are not going to do that."

Skeeter was a friend of his brother's. A bad

friend. Booze, drugs and women. That's what they'd find at Skeeter's boat house.

"I can sleep there," Pierre said, his tone so matter-of-fact, Julien could almost believe he was being sincere.

But no one actually ever *slept* at Skeeter's house. They partied all night instead.

"You'll sleep better in your own bed," Julien said, opening the truck's squeaky door to shove his brother inside.

"Does Mama have any of those good dumplings left?" Pierre asked, his head drooping.

"I'm sure she saved you a whole bowlful. But you might not want to eat too much right now."

"Hungry."

Of course Pierre was hungry. He was always hungry. Julien had to wonder if his brother needed more than just food and drink to sustain him. He also wondered if he needed such sustenance himself.

Maybe they were both hungry for something they couldn't see or touch.

And maybe that was the main reason Julien had decided to change his own wayward ways, right along with his brother's.

Chapter Six

Ramon Blanchard hobbled into the Fleur Café, his soft smile belying the determined look Alma saw in his dark-brown eyes. Her father had always reminded her of a gentle giant. His brawny arms were muscular and work-worn, his craggy face as rich and mapped as the muddy sand bars lining the swamp, his laugh lines crinkled and gouged like a river bluff. His whole countenance was edged with sorrow and his shaggy gray beard curled like Spanish moss around his ample chin, adding to the mystic qualities she so loved.

She'd rather jump into an alligator pond than hurt her dear sweet daddy.

"Daddy's already heard about the kiss," she said in a tight-lipped whisper to Winnie, her hand still on the scrambled eggs and pancakes she needed to take out to a hungry customer.

"Surprised it took him this long to come in for

a look-see," Winnie replied, turning to go back into the kitchen. "He didn't say anything to you at the festival committee meeting?"

Alma shook her head. "No, and no one dared mention it, either."

No one wanted to be around to witness the wrath of Ramon Blanchard. Her father had always been loving but strict, fair but foreboding, but everyone knew he was a sweetheart of a man underneath that gray beard and those frightening, storm-tossed eyes.

All the same, Alma braced herself for a good reaming. No matter that all three of his daughters were grown up and self-sufficient. He still saw them as his *bébés*.

Her daddy spotted her, waited for her to serve her customer, then straddled a stool at the counter and grunted for some coffee.

"Heavy with cream," he said, his voice booming just enough to make the glassware rattle. "And bring me a mess of beignets, too."

Daddy always ordered a mess of beignets and all the workers knew he liked his dark coffee laced with heavy cream. How the man still walked around was beyond Alma. But she'd given up on fussing at him about eating healthily. It only made things worse between them. Let him have his sweets and his coffee.

The young rookie waitress named Mollie

seemed to be the only one oblivious to the undercurrents rushing through the café like flood waters. She brought the coffee and cream and then whirled to take the plate of plump, hot, square-shaped beignets, making sure Mr. Blanchard had extra powdered sugar and a slab of butter to enjoy with his breakfast.

"Anything else, Mr. Blanchard?"

Ramon took a long swig of coffee then cleared his throat. "Yep. You can tell my middle daughter Alma Marie Blanchard to come on out here and say good morning to her papa."

"Of course," Mollie replied with a hesitant smile, her brown hair falling around her face. "She was just right here."

Alma walked out of the kitchen toward her father, feeling like she was walking a plank, the whole restaurant full of people following her every step with squinted brows and lips moving as if in silent prayer.

Deciding to just get it over and done with, Alma put a little bounce in her step. "Hello, Daddy. I was wondering if you were gonna stop by this week."

"I reckon so," Ramon said between bites of golden-fried dough. "I just bet dat you were." He chewed and stewed a couple of seconds. "How ya been, Daughter Number Two?"

She knew she was in trouble since he'd numbered her. They each got a number when he wasn't happy. "Uh…"

"You gonna stand dere squeakin' like a little bird or you gonna talk to your papa?" His Cajun accent was pronounced, another sure sign that he was agitated. But a tightly held grin tried to break through.

Alma almost laughed. Seeing the twinkle in her daddy's big brown eyes gave her such a measure of relief, she had to lean against the counter for support. "I'm fine, Papa. How 'bout you?"

Ramon leaned close, his girth keeping him from making much progress. "Me, I'm fine. Just fine. My phone's tired, though. 'Cause it's been ringing like a Christmas bell for de last few days. Wanna know why?"

"I can't imagine."

"I think you know," Ramon said, wiping his plump fingers on a paper napkin. "In fact, I'm pretty sure de whole town knows why my phone keeps jingling."

"Well, out with it, then," Alma retorted, but it was with a sweet tone so as not to offend.

He waved a hand toward the back door. "Did you kiss Julien LeBlanc dere on the back steps?"

"Yes, sir," Alma said, holding up her finger. "You already know about the kiss, but it's more like *he* kissed me. Caught me off guard."

"*He* kissed *you?*" Ramon took another bite of beignet.

"Yes, sir." She lowered her head, hoping her humility would appease her daddy. That had always worked in high school.

"Well, then if he was the one doing the kissing, I reckon I'd better be having this conversation with him instead of you—since you seem to be so innocent and all."

Alma ignored the whisper of snickers filling the nearby vicinity. Let them all laugh. She was a grown woman.

"I'm a grown woman," she repeated out loud to her daddy. "I could have stopped him."

"Why didn't you?"

She finally looked up at her daddy. His eyes held a warm regard, a kindness tempered with steel. "I don't know. I guess it just surprised me. I mean, Julien and I have managed to remain civil all these years and I'm so used to him teasing me and bothering me, I just never expected the man to grab me up like that and plant one on me. I honestly was too shocked to react."

"Except to kiss him right back, from what I hear," Ramon said, his tone simmering down to below boiling now.

"Yes, I guess I did. And I guess Callie showed you that picture someone snapped and sent out to all the world."

"I don't need to see a picture to tell what's right in front of my eyes. You better be careful with dat one, Alma Marie. Those LeBlanc boys mean trouble. You know that. I didn't like it when you two dated all through school and, even though you are now fully grown and old enough to make your own choices, I still have to worry. That's my job."

"No need to worry about me, Papa," she said, trying to put the image of Julien standing in her yard last night out of her mind. "I can handle Julien LeBlanc."

"Really now? So no need for your tired old papa to give you a lecture on broken hearts and lost promises?"

"No lecture needed here," Alma replied, willing that to be the case. "I've changed since high school. Julien can't ever hurt me again."

It didn't help that the person in question just happened to walk in the door at that very moment.

Julien stopped and glanced around, his brother Pierre slamming into his back. Both brothers glanced at each other and then around the busy café.

Pierre caught the vibe, too. "Did somebody die?"

"Why does everybody always ask me that?"

Julien got over his shock and found an empty booth then tugged his hungover brother into one side while he slid into the other. Aware that people were staring at him then looking toward the counter, Julien saw the reason.

Mr. Blanchard. In the flesh. They had never actually gotten along very well. And things hadn't improved after Julien had pulled that stunt at the prom.

People held grudges around here. Especially Blanchard-type people. If the old man had gotten wind that Julien was trying to get back into Alma's good graces, he would be as mad as a gator with a hook caught in its snout. Maybe more so.

"I'm hungry," Pierre said, holding his head in his hands. "Only that bacon smell is making me feel kind of green."

"What you drank last night is the reason you feel so green," Julien pointed out. He could only deal with one crisis at a time and since his brother was right in front of him, he'd just have to put Alma and her papa out of his mind for now.

The new girl came waltzing up to the table. "Morning."

Pierre must have caught a whiff of her perfume. He looked up and broke out into a grin, green and all. *"Bonjour, belle."* Then he looked at her name tag. "Mollie. Pretty Mollie."

Mollie smiled over at Pierre. First. Even before she smiled at Julien. This was interesting. He should be insulted since his baby brother looked like death warmed over with his dark curls all askew and his onyx eyes bloodshot and unfocused. Why hadn't Mollie noticed Julien's combed hair and clean T-shirt? What did that matter? Julien looked around for another pretty woman.

And saw Alma standing in the kitchen behind the pass-through, her expression stony and steely, her eyes fixed on her daddy. Was she expecting some sort of showdown?

"What can I get for y'all?" Sweet Mollie asked, her gaze still fixed on puny Pierre.

"Your telephone number," Pierre said through a grin.

Mollie giggled. Blushed. Smiled.

Ramon Blanchard grunted.

Alma whirled and walked away.

And Julien sat wondering what his next move might be.

He'd tried flowers. He'd tried tea cakes. Maybe it was time he tried something else. Something that would throw Alma completely off guard.

"I'll be back," he told his suddenly lovesick little brother. Then he looked at Mollie. "Bring him a big pot of black coffee and some dry toast. I'll have a short stack with grits and scrambled eggs."

Pierre's grin almost cracked on that, but he still kept his eyes on Mollie. "Toast sounds good," he said, his words as weak as a newborn puppy's yelp. "I'm feeling kind of poorly this morning."

"I'm sorry for that. I'll be back before you can say boo," Mollie said, her smile reassuring.

"Boo," Pierre replied, testing that theory.

He was rewarded with another giggle.

Julien was already up.

"Where you going?" Pierre asked, panic in his voice.

"Right over there, to speak to Mr. Blanchard."

Pierre's eyes opened wide. "You're crazy, bro."

"*Oui,* I just might be at that."

Alma wasn't a coward. She just didn't need the drama today. She hadn't slept very well and this day was fast going from bad to worse. A worker had called in sick. Her daddy had come to take her to task. Her sisters—one texting and leaving phone messages and the other one waving and grinning and coming in to the café to bother her—and her co-workers were having a ball teasing her about Julien's new interest in her. And now, Julien was—

Sitting down right beside her daddy. Shaking her daddy's hand. Chatting with her daddy. Only, Papa was not chatting back.

"I'm so glad I had the early shift today," Winnie said, poking Alma in the ribs. "I haven't seen this much excitement since old man Gauthier lost his false teeth in his gumbo."

"I'm glad you're being entertained," Alma retorted. "We do have people waiting, you know."

"They ain't going anywhere," Winnie replied. "This is too good. Nobody wants to leave." Then she poked Alma again. "And here comes Callie. Woo-wee, this is the best day ever."

Alma let out a groan. "Easy for you to say."

She moved close to the pass-through, hoping she could hear what Julien was saying to her frowning father. But the buzz of too many interested people blurred out most of Julien's soft-spoken words.

She heard *daughter* and *sorry* and *second chance* and her heart started beating to match that buzz. Was Julien asking her father for permission to…to what? Start all over again? Date Alma? Goodness, did everyone around here think she was still in high school?

Deciding to take matters into her own hands, she hurried out to the counter. "Julien, stop it."

Both her daddy and Julien glanced up.

"Hello, *catin*," Julien said with a warm smile. "I was just telling your papa about the sweet bateau I've been making to display at the festival. Also have a nice skiff and a pirogue, if I get it finished. I wanted to get his opinion so I invited him to come to the warehouse and have a look."

"But I—"

Was she imagining things? Had she heard wrong?

"But what?" Ramon asked, his heavy eyebrows floating together. "He asked me if I'd like to test the water."

Okay, that could mean any number of challenges or confrontations. "How so, Papa?"

"Maybe go crawfishing or trap a gator, like the good old days. Chase a quarry," Julien finished. "If I don't sell the boats at the festival, that is. Thought we'd take one of them out."

"Over at Second Chance Landing," Ramon said, winking at her. "That's prime gator waters there."

Water. Quarry. Second Chance…Landing.

Alma needed to unclog her ears.

Julien's smile was serene, his expression full of pure joy. "I haven't talked to your daddy in a month of Sundays. I aim to make up for that."

Ramon gave Julien a measured look. "I just might take you up on that, son. Chartering deep sea fishing tours is good and all that, but gator hunting wouldn't be nearly as boring."

Alma huffed a breath. "Daddy, you haven't hunted gators in twenty years."

"All the more reason to go for it."

She grasped for something sensible to say. "But Julien's boats are wooden. Don't most people use aluminum boats now?"

"Oui," Julien said. "I can build one of those, too. But a good, solid cedar bateau or pirogue will get the job done today just the same way they did a century ago."

"He wants my opinion," Ramon said, his voice going deep. "On several accounts."

"It's not alligator season," she pointed out.

"All the more reason to be careful what we hook," her daddy replied.

Alma didn't know whether to laugh or cry. "I know you two wouldn't do anything illegal. So what's going on?"

"Nothing for you to worry 'bout," her daddy said through a full-blown Daddy glare. "Business and other man stuff."

"Okay, all right, fine." She glared at both of them. "Do you want a refill, Papa?"

"Me, *non*. I'm fine."

"And I see my food is ready," Julien said, getting up. "Nice talking to you, Mr. Blanchard."

Her papa shook Julien's hand. "I'll be in touch."

"I'm counting on it." Julien saluted and then took off to join his brother.

"That was odd," Callie said as she slid into the booth beside her daddy and gave him a quick kiss on the cheek.

"Yes, it was." Alma looked over at Julien. He looked too smug, too proud.

"What did he really say to you, Daddy?"

"We talked boats and fishing and catching things."

Callie tossed her hair and snorted a giggle. "Seems I got here just in time."

"You're all driving me crazy," Alma retorted, turning to head back into the kitchen. "I have work to do."

Winnie grabbed her by the arm. "What happened?"

"I'm not sure. But I think Julien is taking my daddy gator hunting. Only it's not alligator season."

"No. That's September," Winnie answered, twisting her lips.

"Then how can Julien take my daddy gator hunting?"

Winnie grinned. "Maybe they just made that up to fool you."

"Or maybe I'm just *being* foolish," Alma said. "I thought they were talking about something else."

"Like you, maybe?"

"Well, yes."

Callie came into the kitchen and poured herself some coffee. "Okay, what did I miss? Three people called me to tell me there might be a fight over here between Papa and Julien."

"No, no," Winnie said, trying to explain. "I think they're gonna go out in one of Julien's custom-made boats to look for gators even though it isn't gator season."

"That's illegal," Callie replied, her eyes on Alma. "Unless, of course, they're just looking and not capturing or killing."

"I think it's a cover," Winnie said. "But I think Julien has something else in mind."

Callie bobbed her head. "I think my daddy might be thinking of *feeding* the alligators. We'll know if Julien goes missing."

"I think I'm getting a headache," Alma retorted, turning back to her work. She had coffee to make and orders to take care of and her supply closet needed to be inventoried.

Callie followed her around and leaned close. "I think Julien is hunting for one thing and one thing only. *You.*"

Alma's heart did that funny thing again. "I do feel as if I'm being stalked."

"But in a good way because he's not dangerous," Callie said, grinning.

"Maybe not to you," Alma replied, turning

around to gather more napkins and utensils. "But he could hurt me again. I can't let him do that. And I can't let my daddy get involved either."

"Too late," Callie said. "They just walked out the door together."

Chapter Seven

Julien followed Alma's father out onto the sidewalk. A playful early morning breeze teased the bright red geraniums planted in two clay pots on each side of the double front doors. Alma liked to keep an inviting entryway.

Mr. Blanchard pushed past the pretty flowers then pulled Julien up close against the brick wall between the café and Callie's lush nursery and garden store. "Wanna tell me what you're up to, Julien? 'Cause, me, I'm thinking it's not so much about boats and alligators as it is about messing with me and my second-born daughter. Am I right?"

The man didn't waste words.

"Yes, sir." Julien looked around to make sure his brother was still preoccupied with sweet Mollie. And that no one else was within listening distance. A set of tinkling wind chimes hanging in Callie's garden played a melody in the wind. "I did want you to see my boats…I mean, if you're interested…but I'd like to inform you that I aim to work things out with Alma. And I want to make peace with you while I'm at it."

Ramon put a beefy hand to his ear. "Come again, son?"

"I want to win back Alma."

There, he'd said it. Julien knew it to be true, but how on earth would he ever get past the stone wall of Ramon Blanchard?

Or the stubborn silence of Alma Marie Blanchard?

Or even his own crusty doubts?

Ramon's burly black scowl didn't scare Julien nearly as much as Alma's solid wall of resistance. But he needed her daddy to believe in him again. To really believe in him. Just another part of the revelation that had shadowed him all week.

"You want to fix things with my little Alma?"

"Yes, sir."

"And how you gonna do dat? It's been a few years now and dis is the first I've heard of such nonsense."

"It took me a while to figure things out, sir."

Ramon Blanchard stared over at Julien, his dark eyes as steely and aged as a rusty anchor. "Did you figure out that if you hurt her again I will not only go for a long boat ride into a deep bayou with you, but also I will most assuredly feed you to the alligators myself?"

"Hadn't figured on that, but now that you mention it—"

"I am not playing around here, son," Mr. Blanchard said, his smile stuck in one position for all to see. "My family has been through too much pain over the past few years. And my Alma, she takes things to heart. You only get one chance with her and I'm pretty sure you used yours up when you broke her heart before. I can't let you do that to her again just 'cause you all of a sudden have a hankering to make things right."

"I don't plan to break her heart," Julien replied, his tone low and even. "I never planned to break her heart back then, either." He shrugged, lowered his head. "I got scared back then." He glanced up at Ramon, shocking himself with that admission. "Have you ever wanted something so badly that it just tore you up to think about it? About not having it, about having it and losing it, about messing things up?"

Ramon gave him a slanted look, his aged eyes going dark. "I've loved and lost, but you know that. I know all about pain and regret and heartache. No need to talk in riddles to me. But you did mess up. You'd better mean it this time, is all I can say."

With that, he turned and barreled up the street,

a big, beefy cut of a man with a heart that had been shattered by a piercing grief.

Julien vowed he would not add to that grief.

He turned to go back inside and found Alma staring at him through the window. She hurried out to meet him before he made it to the door.

"What are you doing, talking to my daddy that way?"

Julien cut to the chase. "I told him I aim to win you back."

He watched the little river of doubt, followed by a waterfall of possibilities, flowing through her eyes. "And what did he say about that?"

"He told me he'd kill me if I mess things up."

She smiled, nodded. "I second that."

"Does that mean you're interested?" Julien asked, hoping, even with the threat of death hanging over his head.

"I didn't say that," she retorted, her hands on her hips. "I just know that my daddy means it when he says something. So be very careful, Julien."

"I'm trying," he said. "I want to try, Alma. With you."

She gave him another long look. "We'll have to see. I've taught myself to not trust you. Taught myself to just ignore you. I'm finding it hard to believe you've had such a swift change of heart."

"My heart never changed," he blurted out. "But my head was a tad confused."

She looked skeptical. "So just like that, you want to go back to the past?"

"No, just like that I want to look toward the future."

"Has that worked? This trying to forget the past? Has it worked for you because I sure have a hard time letting bygones be bygones."

"I didn't forget the good parts with you," he said, thinking he'd have to be honest with her. "I blew it back then, projecting my worst fears on myself by acting like a mule. But time is precious, Alma. We both know that. Life is a gift. I'm tired of wasting it." He shrugged, pushed at the curls mushing over his forehead. "We've wasted time, you and me. We can be friends—I don't mind that one bit. But while we're being friends, I just wish you'd consider me. Consider more with me."

She stood still, as still as she'd been that early morning in the restaurant. "Considering more with you could break my heart, Julien."

"I am not going to break your heart," he said, grounding the words out. "I wish everybody would quit saying that."

She looked sheepish. "I reckon I'm not being fair. I'm supposed to forgive those who trespass against me."

"That's what the good book suggests, *oui*."

"I can't ignore you," she said, her tone soft and silky and almost forgiving. "You're a good customer and you supply me with a lot of my seafood. We have nice *working* relationship. I appreciate that, at least."

"But…I want more, Alma."

"I still don't get why you all of a sudden decided this."

He couldn't tell her that seeing her so sad had only reinforced his mother's wishes and his heart's deeply buried desires.

"It's just time," he said, hoping that would hold her off for a while. "Past time."

"What if I find somebody else before I decide about you?"

Wondering if she already had, he said, "That would break *my* heart."

"You'd get over it," she said. Then she turned to go back inside. "I'm gonna have to think about this. I'll see you later, Julien."

"Okay."

He didn't know whether that was a good sign or a bad one. *Later* could mean a number of things. "Are you going to the festival meeting tonight?" he asked.

"I'm on the committee," she replied, letting the door shut behind her.

"I'll take that for a yes, then."

Pierre came strolling out, a to-go cup full of coffee in one hand. "I have a date with Pretty Mollie Friday night."

"You sure work fast," Julien said, thinking his little brother's love life was always right on time.

"She's a sweet girl," Pierre said, squinting before he jabbed his fancy sunshades onto his nose. "Goes to our church."

Julien lifted the shades to stare at his brother. "Our church? Since when do you even know the way to our church?"

"I'm going Friday night," Pierre said, "with Mollie."

Julien watched his brother walk toward the truck then lifted both his hands in the air. "Thank you, Lord."

It was a small step in the right direction for Pierre. And maybe another sign for Julien. An inspiration for him to keep fighting the good fight. These past few days had been loaded with signs from above. What next? A knock on his hard head?

Julien turned to stare back inside the café, watching as Alma and Winnie laughed and whispered, watching as Pretty Mollie served the customers with a kind smile and Callie walked around chatting with everyone. He liked how the Fleur Café was a gathering place for the people who lived here, a place where someone in a hurry could serve himself and leave his money or an IOU note on the counter. He liked that Alma kept fresh flowers from her sister's nursery all around. Alma had a way of making people feel welcome with good food and fine fellowship. She'd always welcomed him, in spite of her harsh feelings toward him. She'd never once turned him away and she could have. Should have.

But that was Alma. Good and kind. Hardworking and trustworthy. Beautiful and pure. She'd stayed here, even after he'd broken her heart, because her family had needed her.

Would she stay here just because he needed her?

That would be the test.

Julien took one last look at the comforting scene inside the café and then turned to get on with his day.

Lord, help me to make this work, he prayed. *Help my little brother to get back right with You. And help me to get back right with Alma.*

Julien figured if he could make everything right in his little world and settle down with Alma, not only would his dear mother be pleased but so would the Lord.

And it might ease his own pent-up grief about losing his father.

A tall order for a man who'd played at life and played just about everyone in his life. The image of his father lying in his boat with a four-hundred-pound alligator dead beside him came front and center into Julien's mind.

His father had asked him to go out with him that day, but Julien had been hungover and surly and he'd wanted to work on his first attempt at building a boat. Later in the day, his mother had questioned him, asking him to go and take his daddy some lunch. And that's when Julien had found his papa, tucked away in what he called his secret hunting place.

Dead.

He'd wrestled that gator into the boat all by himself.

And it had killed him. Not the gator. His daddy had shot the monster after he'd hooked him. But somebody had to haul the alligator in. Edward LeBlanc was a renowned alligator hunter, had done that job for most of his life. It was just that his heart had given up. But he hadn't. At least not before he'd hauled in his prize.

Julien closed his eyes, the image of his stubborn, determined daddy grunting with each hefty lift of that big old alligator clear in his mind. If he'd been there, if he'd helped, his daddy might still be alive today. But Edward LeBlanc didn't give up on his catch.

That was just how people around here did things. Even in death, the people of Fleur knew how to make a grand exit.

At the funeral, all of his papa's friends had hailed him as a hero and a conqueror. "Dead beside that gator," one friend lamented. "Ain't dat just like Edward to bring in a record-breaking twelve footer, even when he had one foot toward the Pearly Gates and one foot in the fire?"

Julien had mourned his daddy's death. They all had. The whole town. Alma had sent food and visited with his mother and hugged him close, her eyes full of pain and anger and questions.

That hug had stayed with Julien that night after she'd left. And now the memory held him again. He remembered her pretty dress and the scent of lemons and wisteria. He remembered wanting to run after her and ask her to wrap her arms around him and hold him for a long, long time.

But she'd left.

And the days turned into months and the months into almost a half year now. Julien had worked hard since then. So hard that he fell into bed tired at night. Tired and lonely and grieving.

Was he finally having the meltdown he'd held back for so long?

Was he allowed that? No, LeBlancs didn't melt. They didn't give in. They just wrestled until the finish.

Julien knew he was in the wrestling match of his life.

He aimed to win.

"He seems determined," Callie pointed out to Alma back in the café. "I mean, he talked to Papa. That took guts."

"Julien has always had nerve," Alma replied, her hands busy breaking lettuce for salad. "Sometimes, though, he rushes into things without thinking them through."

Callie watched the unfortunate lettuce being shredded, bit by bit. "You think he's being impulsive, wanting to make things right with you? He's had a long time to think about that, Alma."

Alma stopped, grabbed a juicy tomato to put in the salad, her efficient knife slicing and dicing perfect chunks of the home-grown Big Boys. "I think he's going through something. He thinks it involves me. But maybe it just involves him coming to terms with things."

"Such as?"

"His daddy's death. It's coming up on a year now this fall. But spring's here now and that was always a busy time for Mr. Edward and his sons. Julien took it pretty hard but it's like a wound that heals over itself, only underneath the wound never really goes away. I think the coming season and his daddy's birthday has brought out all his angst and grief."

Callie's eyes went dark. "I think we all have those kind of seasons."

Alma gritted her teeth against her sister's faraway look. "That's why I can't be mean to Julien. I've been so wrapped up in my own doubts and worries, I don't think I've given him a proper Christian attitude of forgiveness."

Callie slapped at her arm then grabbed a carrot

and starting chopping it. "Sweetie, I don't think he's got you having a proper Christian attitude on his mind right now."

"Stop it," Alma said, grinning in spite of her red cheeks. "I haven't thought of Julien in that way in a long, long time."

"Never? Really never?" Callie asked, her knife pointing in the air. "Not once since y'all broke up?"

"Okay, maybe every now and then. It's hard to forget. He was so…different. Such a sweet talker, so…bad. So not my type." So much her type, Alma silently corrected.

"Yeah, we all remember that part."

"But there was good in him, even back then. I think the good's overtaking the bad in him now. He's wrestling with things, trying to fight the devil at the crossroads."

"What about all those other women he's supposedly dated?"

Alma stilled. She couldn't be jealous. And she couldn't think about Julien with someone else. "I haven't seen him with anybody in a while now."

Callie leaned close. "Alma, you're kind of defending the man. What's up with that?"

"I don't know," Alma admitted. "He's just… different lately. I think he's worried about his mama and his brother and it's like looking into a mirror. His prior actions are now being emulated by Pierre. We all know that boy loves his big brother."

"And Julien's the only male role model he has now."

"Exactly. So maybe he's not so much wanting to get closer to me as he's wanting to make a better impression on his brother. I'm all for helping Pierre, but I don't like being used in that way."

"You could be a part of that," Callie said, obviously glad to have something dramatic and romantic to gnaw on. "You could help him make a difference in his brother's life."

"I could." Alma finished the big salad and quickly covered it in plastic wrap for the lunch crowd. "I could. But I don't want to give Julien false hope. I can't pretend. It wouldn't be fair."

"What if you weren't pretending?"

"What do you mean?"

Callie snared a carrot and started chewing on it. "What if you actually did give Julien LeBlanc another chance?"

Chapter Eight

Her sister's suggestion floored Alma.

She'd been fighting Julien at every turn, determined to keep him at arm's length. That self-imposed self-control had been her edge over the past few years, had kept her sane and settled. Because after she'd refused his initial tries at getting her back after the disastrous prom night, Julien had backed off and left her alone for the most part. Maybe because Alma had told him in no uncertain terms that she refused to even think about him until he'd cleaned up his act and grown up.

Then came her mother's illness. She'd focused all of her energy and prayers on that, which gave a girl plenty of reason not to think about a lost love. Except maybe in the wee hours of the night when she'd lie in her bed and let the silent tears trail down her cheeks, tears for her mother, tears for her family and tears for that lost love.

But now, because of his father's death and maybe because he'd suddenly seen his own mortality bright and clear, Julien had gone and ramped up his presence in her life, had stated loud and clear that he was going to make an aggressive assault on her sensibilities. And it seemed to be working, whether she liked it or not.

But that kiss… And the way he seemed to see her for the first time in a long time, the way he looked at her now. Had he always looked at her that way and she'd just been too stupid to see it? Or had she only longed for this?

No, he'd dated other woman, or so she thought. Had he been trying to meet her standards all of this time and now he'd finally realized he was there? Had he tried and failed to get on with his life, the same way she'd tried and failed?

"I can't think about this now," she told Callie, her hands grasping for some busy work. "I think I'll make a Doberge cake. I haven't made one of those in a long time. Should I make chocolate or lemon? Or a mixture?"

Callie grabbed Alma's hand. "That's Julien's favorite dessert."

Alma let out a gasp. "I made one for him after…after his father died." She turned and put a hand to her brow. "Oh, I might be in trouble."

"You can make the cake," Callie said, her tone gentle. "Sell it to your customers. Get it out of your system. But whatever you do, don't take this cake to Julien."

"Why?" Alma asked, afraid of the answer.

"It would make you just as impulsive as him," Callie replied. "It's a big step, thinking about Julien again. He was your first love. Take this slow, Alma. Don't look at it as your last chance."

She whirled to glare at her sister. "What do you mean by that?"

"You know what I mean. Julien is locked in here in Fleur."

Alma lifted a hand into the air. "And I'm not?"

"You could easily go. Just go and travel and explore and try to open your own restaurant in New Orleans or Atlanta or anywhere you've ever dreamed about."

"I'm not so sure about that now. It's hard to start a business from scratch these days. And I can't leave Papa."

"You could. Papa would send you with his blessings and some start-up cash."

"But we both know he's hurting. I couldn't leave him now." She turned to look for the flour. "And I certainly can't leave this place."

"Winnie could take over as your manager," Callie suggested. "She's been here practically since the beginning. Mama trained her."

Alma knew that, had considered it many times. Winnie had always been her relief, the one she turned to when she couldn't make it in to work, which was rare. "I'm not ready to let go."

Callie leaned close, the buzz of people moving and talking around them humming to a dull roar. "Maybe you're *afraid* to let go."

Then Callie gave her a peck on the cheek and walked away.

Alma stood there holding the flour container, the sound of dishes clinking together playing in perfect harmony with the sizzle of bacon and the hiss of pancakes hitting the griddle.

I want to leave, Lord, she prayed. *I want to just go and run and keep on running. I want to be away, far away from my pain and my guilt and my worries about what the future might bring. But...I can't let go. I can't. Mama loved this café. And I loved Mama. I can't break my daddy's heart again. Help me, Lord. Help me to accept that this might be my calling.*

And what if this was her calling? Could she settle for that?

Alma hurried to the refrigerator and grabbed eggs and butter, her actions automatic and ingrained, like the tide flowing in and out of the gulf. But inside, her mind was in turmoil, a raging storm of worry and wonder that threatened her safe, solid existence. And she was afraid that storm was going to hit sooner than later and change her world into something she wasn't ready to face.

Unless she found a way to keep it at bay.

She baked the Doberge cake, and took it to the festival committee meeting.

"You brought a dobash cake?" Mayor Denny Daigle said, using the locals' name for the cake. "Man, I love me some of that."

Alma sliced him a piece, the seven layers of cake and creamy pudding as beautiful on the inside as the chocolate fondant covering the outside. "Here you go, Mr. Mayor."

"Hmm." Denny grabbed a fork and dug in, his lips smacking with each bite.

Frances LaBorde came up and sniffed at the cake. "Looks mighty good, Alma. Is it a special occasion?"

"No, I was just in the mood to bake," Alma replied, her gaze cast down.

Then she glanced up and saw Julien coming toward her, his swagger intact, his jeans clean and fitting just right, his button-up shirt pressed and crisp. His hair, always so dark and wild, was brushed and shiny. But one rascal of a curl dipped over his dark brows like an enticing question mark.

Her heart went as soft as the creamy pudding

holding the cake together. Mercy, what was happening to her?

Julien looked at the cake instead of her. "Is that a dobash cake?"

"Sure is," Reverend Guidry said through a grin and a bite. "Alma, this is as good as my dear grandmama's dobash. You have to make this more often."

Alma couldn't speak. Her throat was dry, her hands sweaty.

Julien's gaze slinked up from the cake to her face. "Looks so good."

"Would you like a slice?"

"You know I would," he said, his gaze lingering over her lips.

Alma wouldn't let her hand tremble as she cut into the moist, rich cake. She held steady as she slapped the fat slice down on a paper plate. She refused to look up as she handed it to Julien.

His fingers brushed hers and a warmth seemed to seep into her very bones. "Thank you, Alma."

She finally gave in and lifted her head, her gaze searching for him. Big mistake. The icing covering that cake didn't have nearly the richness of Julien's beautiful chocolate eyes. He gave her a long stare, a serious look that held her.

"You're welcome," she squeaked out.

Julien found a seat then poured a cup of coffee and sat silently eating his cake. His stony quietness was even more disconcerting than his teasing and flirting, Alma decided.

What was he up to now?

What was she up to, baking this cake?

Alma knew how much Julien loved a good Doberge cake. He always went to the original Doberge Bakery when he was in New Orleans so he could bring home a cake.

But Alma's version was every bit as good as the original, for sure. He watched her while he savored each bite. She'd baked this cake today, right after he'd talked to her daddy.

To torment him?

Or to send him a definite message?

Hmm, maybe both.

He chewed on that while he enjoyed the cake. Then he held his plate up. "I'd like another slice, please."

Alma's smile was so soft, it reminded him of water lilies floating in a hush on a pond. And choked him in the same way those pretty lilies could choke a bayou.

He reached for the second, bigger slice, his fingers deliberately touching hers, his eyes holding her as she gasped and drew her hand back then shot him a stern look.

He took a big bite, enjoying the moist cake against the creamy pudding while enjoying watching her blush and take her seat.

Two could play this game. It seemed Alma was one of the two now. A first step. A little dance of acceptance, even while her eyes denied she'd taken up the gauntlet.

"Cela devrait être amusant."

"What did you say, Julien?" Frances asked, her eyes bright with interest.

"I said this meeting should be fun. I'm all about the festival."

He winked at Alma.

She started scribbling in her neat little notebook.

"Where's your daddy?" Frances asked Alma, her tone just above desperate.

"He should be here," Alma said, her words quiet and firm.

Frances checked the door then let out a sigh. "Well, let's get started, shall we?"

Frances had been trying to get Alma's daddy to notice her since the day she'd delivered a big pot of jambalaya after the funeral. Julien had noticed the flirtation and he knew it bothered Alma. A lot seemed to be bothering Alma tonight.

He hoped he was first in line.

Frances shuffled through her notes. "First up—the *cochon de lait.*"

Alma looked up and right at Julien. "I can report on the pig roast, Miss Frances."

So maybe she wasn't playing after all, Julien thought. Except to insult him, of course.

"I'd be glad to help with that," Julien said, forgetting he was already in charge of popcorn and...he couldn't remember what else.

"You're already in charge of popcorn, cotton candy and funnel cakes," Miss Frances kindly reminded him. "We don't want to overburden you your first year as a committee member."

Julien nodded. "Okay, then."

"Would you like to give your report?" Frances asked, seeming to forget the pig roast.

Everyone waited while Julien realized he didn't have a report. "I don't have a report."

Alma rolled her eyes and tapped her pen on the table. "We explained this at the last meeting. You need to get volunteers lined up. You need to talk to Reverend Guidry about the machines and supplies. You need to set up a schedule."

"And you need to be writing this down," Frances added, her look of disapproval aimed squarely at Julien.

Alma tore a piece of paper out of her notebook with a bit too much zest and shoved it toward him. "Do you have a pen?"

"Here, son," the reverend said, shaking his head and grinning. "I'll help you since I have the equipment and I'll show you how to mix everything so you don't get popcorn in the cotton candy, at least."

"Thank you," Julien said, sitting up to look interested. "I'll get it all together. I know I'm supposed to get some of the young people to help, right?"

"That's right," the reverend replied. "I've already mentioned it to our youth director. She's made a schedule so the kids can see when they need to report to your booth."

Julien wrote that down. "Check. Youth already have a schedule."

"Good," Frances said. "We expect well over five thousand people on festival day."

"Five thousand people?" Julien frowned. "That's a lot of popcorn." Wouldn't leave him much time to follow Alma around.

"Now you're getting the picture," Alma replied. "This is serious business. It brings tourists to our town and puts dollars into the local economy— something we all need to be serious about."

Well, she'd certainly put him in his place.

"I get that," Julien said. "That's why I'm here. Now back to that pig roast…"

Ramon Blanchard walked up just in time to scowl at Julien. "I'll be glad to roast a pig."

"Like father, like daughter," Julien mumbled.

Alma offered more cake slices to the committee members, including Julien. Kissing her reticent father good night, she headed off to her house, her nearly empty cake carrier tucked underneath her arm.

Until two strong hands lifted it away from her body. "Why do you always walk home alone? It's not safe."

Julien.

Her heart took off faster than her feet.

Finding her voice, she retorted, "I live across the street."

"It's still not safe."

"I know the neighborhood."

"I worry about you."

Alma stopped, looking both ways. She'd hate to push him out in front of a car. "You mean you worry about me since you had some kind of revelation? I've been just fine for oh, a long time now. So fine that you've hardly noticed."

"I've always worried," he admitted. Then he escorted her across the empty street. "Why did you bake me a cake?"

She stopped again, back on the safe side of the sidewalk. "I didn't bake you a cake. I baked a cake to serve at the festival meeting and you had a piece or two there."

"And you knew I'd be there."

"Actually, I wasn't sure you'd be there. You're not that dependable."

She knew she'd hit home in the way his expression shifted into the shadows. Why did she have to be so mean all of a sudden?

"I took notes this time," he replied. He hit his pocket where he'd tucked the paper inside. "I know my responsibilities and I won't let you down."

"I'm counting on you, so I hope you mean that. But you wouldn't be letting me down. We're all in this together, you know. We need all the help we can get. Last year was hard, what with storms and oil spills and such. We're slowly coming back to life around here."

"*Oui,* and that's exactly how I feel. As if I'm finally coming back to life. Can you understand that, Alma?"

"I want to." Trying again, she said, "You can keep the rest of the cake."

He pointed to the foil-wrapped package he'd placed on top of the cake carrier. "You already gave me a share."

His tone was so innocent and sweet, Alma melted a little bit. "Take the rest to your mama and Pierre." Then because she did have a heart, she asked, "How are they?"

He looked up then, his dark eyes testing her. Letting out a breath, he shrugged. "Not so good, *chère.* Not so good."

Alma knew she was stepping over a line. But she was caught in a snare, and the tangled web of longing in her memories was holding her tight. "Would you like to come in for some coffee, Julien?"

He shifted the big plastic cake carrier around so he wouldn't drop it, then stood silent for a minute. Then he gave her a crooked half-smile that seemed tinged with a weariness she'd never noticed before. "That would be nice, if you're sure."

Alma nodded then turned toward her house. The night wind hummed around her and the sound of her sister's chimes playing next door sang a sweet, melodious warning. But she kept walking, unable to turn him away. Not tonight. Not after he'd finally been honest with her about something.

And especially not after she'd baked him a cake.

Chapter Nine

Julien watched as she turned on lights and kicked off her shoes. Alma had dainty, tiny feet and shapely legs. Her skirt flirted around her knees like a flower petal. Her pretty cotton top had a giant butterfly spreading his wings across the front.

He thought of poems and flowers, of moonlight and fireflies. He couldn't believe she'd asked him in, not only inside her home, but maybe into her heart just a little tiny bit. He had to tread lightly or he'd be out on his nose again.

"I'll get the coffee going," she said, moving around in the kitchen, nervous energy driving her. "Have a seat."

Julien settled down on a high-backed sofa and took in the vast array of colors surrounding him. Fresh flowers everywhere. Lilies, wisteria, jasmine, spilling out of tall vases. Cushions made of old quilt pieces of rich reds, forest greens and sky blues. Cast-off furniture she'd taken and re-worked into shiny white with flowers and lady-bugs painted on them. A white table and old, mismatched chairs, all painted and embellished in a whimsical, welcoming way.

The kitchen was small but clean and tidy. The bright colors carried into that room, too. Red pots and pans mingled with blue enamel and hand-made pottery. A heavy yellow biscuit bowl held fresh fruit. Alma loved to support the local art-ists.

The smell of strong coffee tickled at his nose, making him wonder why he'd never taken the time to really look at this dollhouse before.

Because you were too busy trying to show Alma that you were okay without her.

But he wasn't okay. He knew that now. He knew that this place felt like home, at long last.

"Are you okay?" she asked, sitting down beside him on the wide old couch. She fluffed her skirt and tossed some pillows between them. Still hold-ing onto her barriers.

Julien swallowed, wondered how to answer. He plucked at the lace on a cushion. "I don't know. I mean, I know you think I've hit my head or some-thing. It's hard to explain."

"What, Julien?" She appeared sincere, concerned, mystified. "You and I, we've always respected each other. Even after..."

"Even after I behaved so badly?"

She gave him a soft smile. "Yes. I could never be unkind to you, no matter what. And I'm sorry if I've sounded mean lately. You've just taken me by surprise."

His heart spilled open like a flooded river. He knew in that instant—this was why he still loved her. Because she was so kind to everyone. Because she always put other people's needs ahead of her own. Alma was the best example of a true Christian he'd ever seen. She served with a cheerful, grateful heart. He wished he could be more like her.

"You have never been unkind to anyone, *chère*."

She got up and went to the coffeepot then filled two big green mugs with black coffee. "I think I have. I didn't want to like you anymore. I could tolerate you at a distance, even tolerate your teasing and flirting because I knew it meant nothing. But now—"

Amazed that she remembered how he liked his coffee black, Julien took the cup she offered him, the yellow daisies edging the rim amusing him. "Thank you. But now, things have changed. I'm getting too close, right?"

"Yes." Alma sat back down, her own cup

held tightly in both hands. "Now tell me what's really wrong."

Everything. "Why do you think anything is wrong?"

"Because after close to ten years, you've decided you want me back."

"Stranger things have happened."

"Not to me. Not with you." She placed her cup on the grapevine table by the sofa.

"Do you not want me here, Alma?"

She stared over at him, her eyes moving over his face with a brilliant intensity. "There have been many times I wanted nothing more."

That held his heart, tightening it. "And other times?"

"I wanted anything but."

"So you're confused," he said. Then he put his cup next to hers on the glass-topped table. "I have to admit, so am I."

Alma touched a hand to his arm, the feel of her delicate fingers on his skin branding him with a sweet longing. "You've been out there on your own for a while now. We've stayed friends and I've never once tried to change that. I settled for having you nearby, Julien. Nearby, but not too close." She paused, her eyelashes fluttering. "Maybe you think this is all about you and me, but it could be about something else. Something more important."

"What do you mean?"

"You turned away from the church. Maybe it's time you come back."

So she was going to preach to him about his evil ways? He got up to pace in front of the petite fireplace, the brightness of this little room suddenly stifling him. "This has nothing to do with my faith, Alma. I haven't turned away from God." He shrugged, bent his head. "But I did feel unworthy to be near Him at times. And I felt the same about being around you. Just because I don't grace the church with my presence doesn't mean I don't communicate with the Lord."

"Okay, then we can rule that out." She sounded relieved but doubtful. "Did something happen to you recently, something that made you think you want me back in your life?"

Frustrated and tired of being grilled, Julien huffed. "Why does something have to happen to make me finally see what I lost? Why is this so hard to understand?"

She got up to come and stand beside him. "I want to understand, Julien. Really I do. Things happened and we just drifted apart. And now you're back in a big way."

He'd never drifted, he thought. But she had certainly put a levee-strength wall between them. "We didn't work at it, did we?"

She lowered her head. "No. We gave up. I gave

up. I thought you wanted someone else, or something else, besides me."

He pulled her close, his hands holding her waist. "I never gave up, Alma. I just retreated. We settled into a nice, uncomplicated truce. But that truce is over."

With that, he lowered his head to kiss her. Without an audience. His heart opened to her, allowing, asking her to come inside.

He waited and felt her relax against him, heard her almost silent sigh. Her arms pulled around his shoulders, her hands moved up to tug into his hair. Their feelings for each other deepened. He could feel it pouring through him like cleansing water—her acceptance, her forgiveness, her longing. Was this how it felt to be washed in God's forgiveness?

Finally, Alma lifted away, her eyes wide and bright, her expression both shocked and exhilarated. "I guess the cake worked, then."

Julien laughed and kissed her forehead. "*Chère,* it was more than just that cake, but I have to agree. It was sweet and smooth, same as you, Alma."

She took his hands in hers. "You still haven't told me about your mama and Pierre. I want to know. I want to help."

Julien realized that while he believed in kissing his way home, the way to Alma's heart involved honesty and full disclosure. She wanted to hear his feelings. She needed to glimpse his soul. Womanly things were always complicated.

He'd held back from that all those years ago, too prideful to be honest. If he'd told her all of his fears long ago, they might have been able to work things out. Or she might have quit speaking to him entirely. Would that do him in again this time?

"Julien, I'm here and I'm listening. You have my attention."

"Why can't we just be together?" he said, waylaying the heavy thud of his heart. Manly things were a lot less complicated.

She backed away and already he missed her.

"It's not that simple," she retorted as she gathered their cups and took them into the kitchen. "We were together before, remember? But you didn't like the idea of me having a life, of me leaving Fleur." She turned, a hand on the counter. "And if I allow this—you being back in my life—it could happen again. I'd settle for staying here. I'd feel obligated to give in and settle down because—"

"Settle?" He stomped close and stared down at her, his own long-held fury radiating as her words echoed his very fears. "Is that what being with me is all about, Alma? Settling?"

She put a hand to her mouth. "No, I didn't mean that. I just meant—"

"I think I know what you meant," he said, turning toward the door. "I don't want you to settle for me or for my way of life. But you're right about one thing—the same thing that caused me to do you wrong before—*that* is still between us, for sure. I love my life here, my family, my work. But I guess you're just hanging around, biding your time until something or someone better comes along and sweeps you right off your pretty little feet." He stomped back, a finger in the air. "Well, I'm no prince, Alma. I'm not a knight in shining armor. He stopped, inhaled a breath. "Never mind. Just never mind. Maybe I have gone daft, after all, even to hope."

With that, he was out the door, slamming it shut with such a force, the dishes in the pie safe rattled.

Julien stopped underneath the cypress tree, one hand scrubbing across the ancient bark. What had he been thinking? Why had he even begun to hope? Alma, as beautiful and sweet and caring as she was, had a flaw he'd somehow managed to overlook.

The woman was stubborn. And unforgiving. Make that two flaws.

And she wanted more. She wanted better. She

wanted to see what that green grass on the other side was all about.

Make that three or four flaws, tops.

He took a deep breath, willing himself to go home. Just go home and forget the whole deal. Just go back to the way things were before he'd stepped over that line she'd drawn in the sand between them. He'd had a passable life a couple of weeks ago, back when he went through the motions of being a man.

But there was no going back now. Now, he hurt with a furious need that felt like a hook caught in his gill. This was a long dormant pain that had now festered and changed into a certain agony that needed some relief, some healing.

You were so close, he thought. So close. You kissed her, held her, made her see, made her feel again. Made yourself hope again. So close.

He stared up at the little house, at the light still burning inside. Then he watched as that light flickered and went out.

And left him standing there in the darkness.

Without his dobash cake. And without the woman who'd baked it for him.

Inside, Alma stumbled toward the bedroom, shock and realization coloring the darkness with old ghosts and new doubts. The moonlight chased her, glaring a harsh light of accusation on her.

Her sister had warned her she might be settling if she tried to turn back to Julien. He'd figured it out right away, in spite of their sweet kisses and earnest conversation.

Or at least he *thought* she'd be settling. The same way he'd thought that the night of the prom when he'd stood there, reeling on his feet, slurring his insults and accusations, while he tried to justify why he'd turned to another girl.

"You ask too much, Alma. You want too much. You say you want me but you also want to leave our home. You can't have both. It's me or the road."

But she'd never taken to that road. She's stalled out and stayed right here, all the time wondering why Julien didn't come and take her away. Now he'd come back but she was still so afraid of letting him capture her heart. If she gave in and allowed herself to love Julien, would she be trapped here forever? Trapped? Or grounded? Settled? Centered?

Were they destined to self-sabotage any chance they might have at happiness together? Or were they ill-suited for each other to begin with?

Alma sank down on the bed, held her fingers together. "Dear God, is this a sign to let him go? Have I been holding on to him for so long I can't let go?"

Julien had played around with lots of women.

But he'd always come around to see her, each and every day, like clockwork. And she'd lived for those moments, even though she fought those moments, too. Fought and held him at bay, while she secretly relished each glance, each touch, each word.

"Dear Lord, what kind of person am I to do that to him?"

She hurried to get her pajamas on, brushed her teeth, washed her face, combed her hair. She did all the normal, mundane things that she did every night before bed.

Then she kneeled and said a prayer for Julien.

"I know he needs You, Lord. He might have reached out to me, but…I'm pretty sure I messed up on that. Maybe he's really reaching back toward You through me. Please, help him. Keep him strong. And don't let him give up."

Not yet. Not until she'd had a chance to make amends.

She needed to prove to Julien and everyone around here that she wasn't so shallow as to cut and run. She'd stayed after storms, after death, after all sorts of setbacks and tragedies.

"I stayed," she said into the moonlight. "Hasn't anybody seen that? I stayed here."

When I wanted to go. Or so she thought. Did she want to get away from Fleur? Did she really?

Or had she been the one wanting to stay?

Alma looked at the clock. Too late to call Callie or Brenna. She wished she could talk to her mother. Mama would know what to say, would give her advice without judging her. But Mama wasn't here. And her sisters had their own lives.

You are not alone.

Alma lay there in the darkness and heard the soothing words. No, she wasn't alone. She had the Lord. She'd always turned to God for the answers to the hard to explain questions.

And this one ranked right up there.

"Why, God?" she asked, her fingers clutching the floral sheets. "Why did Julien force me to see all my flaws? To see how wrong I've been all these years? How can I change? How can I prove that I'm not going to settle for anything? I have everything I need right here."

And how could she possibly change his perspective on those flaws?

Because now that they'd come so close, she wanted more.

Much more.

Chapter Ten

Julien's cell phone growled rudely near his right ear. Groaning, he flipped over in bed and ran a hand through his hair.

His mother calling at five in the morning?

Not good. Even though he lived in a garage apartment behind her house, he'd always told her to call his cell in an emergency.

He sat up, grabbed the phone. *"Maman?"*

"Your brother's been arrested. You have to go help him, Julien."

Okay, he was wide-awake now. "What happened?" And why had Pierre called Mama instead of him?

"Drinking. Driving drunk." He heard a sob, pictured his mother holding her hand to her heart. "That boy is gonna be the death of me."

"Not if I kill *him* first," Julien retorted.

"I don't need you to kill him. Just try to get

him out of jail." His mother lapsed into Cajun French. Vivid Cajun French.

"Did he hurt anyone?"

"No. But he didn't pass the test. You know, he couldn't walk a straight line or hold his finger to the nose on his face. And apparently that boy has lost possession of his brain, too."

"I'm on my way," Julien said, grabbing clothes.

He didn't doubt that his brother had probably been drunk, but the locals had a thing about getting bored and chasing down drivers. Fleur had a reputation as being a speed trap. He wondered as he drove through the quiet streets if his brother was being singled out for standing out. Pierre was already on the local law enforcement's radar. This would put him front and center on their "most watched" list.

No matter. The boy didn't need to be drinking and driving.

That was not so good.

Julien passed the Fleur Café, his bad mood going to worse. The lights were on and the crew was moving around, about to begin their day. He thought about Alma and that kiss, that *accepting* kiss. She'd let him in, for a brief time, to glimpse what might have been. What might could be. That's all he had to go on right now.

He zoomed on toward the hole-in-the-wall

three-man police station. How this place even had room for a jail cell was beyond Julien's comprehension. But there sat his dour-faced brother in the holding tank, his clothes rumpled and dirty, his expression rumbly and fighting mad.

"I wasn't that drunk," Pierre said by way of a greeting.

"Drunk is drunk, bro," Julien replied, his hands on the steel bars between them. "I'm gonna talk to Chief Watson, okay?"

"I'll be here waiting," Pierre shot back. "Hey, this ain't the Holiday Inn, know what I mean?"

"I should just let him stew," Julien told the chief as he entered the office.

Chief Frank Watson cleared his throat and glanced across the one-room police office into the one-room jail. "Yep. Might do the boy some good."

"What happened?" Julien asked, grumpy from lack of sleep and no coffee.

The chief, a tall, quiet man, got up and poured two cups of rich-as-roux coffee. Handing one to Julien, he said, "Well, we tracked him out near the Backwater."

"Of course."

"Boy was weaving left and right of the center line, tapping his brakes, just driving crazy. My officer felt there was probable cause to stop your brother." He swigged his coffee. "Good thing, too. Pierre slammed on the brakes so hard, he skidded off the road."

Julien was thankful Pierre didn't run off the road. "Did he hurt anyone?"

The sheriff gave him a solemn frown. "No, son. Not this time."

"So what do I do now?" Julien asked, thinking he'd like to throttle his hardheaded brother.

"You can pay his bail and take him home. Course, he's been booked on a misdemeanor charge. He'll need to set a hearing and he'll have to go before a judge and pay some fines. Since this is his first offense, he might get off easy, depending on the judge. He might get probation and community service instead of jail time. I took his license but he'll be issued a temporary one just for things such as going to work and back."

Julien held two fingers to his nose, pushing at the headache forming across his temple. "I'll take care of the bail."

The chief nodded. "Only because your daddy was a friend to this office, I cut the boy some slack. Out of respect for him, I'll release your brother to you. But you are responsible for him, hear me? That means keeping him on the straight and narrow and making sure he shows up for his hearing and court date."

"Which will be?"

"Can't predict, but like I said, if you request a hearing within fifteen days, you can get him into probation and community service. No jail time since it's his first offense and he was barely over the limit. You might want to get a lawyer."

Julien didn't have money for a lawyer or higher insurance rates or any fees—all the things were adding up in his tired brain. But he knew he'd find a way. He had a wad of cash in his pocket for the bail. So much for saving up. "I'll take care of him, Chief Watson. I appreciate your help."

"Kid just needs to lay off the liquor," the chief said as he grabbed a set of heavy keys and headed toward the holding cell. After unlocking the door, he said, "Pierre, your brother is gonna take you home now. I want you to promise me you won't do this again. You need to stop drinking. Your mama can't take this kind of stress, you hear?"

Pierre shot a red-eyed stare toward the chief then darted past him without a word.

"Don't think he enjoyed our luxury suite," the chief said with a knowing smile.

"I hope he remembers this next time he even considers taking a drink," Julien replied. He nodded to the chief and the two other officers then went out to his truck.

The sun was lifting over the bayou, a white-gold orb of beaming light surrounded by a shield of creamy yellow and burnished gold. He'd planned to go shrimping this morning. No need to change those plans. There was still time.

Pierre sat hunched on the passenger side. "I need sleep."

"You need a swift kick in your posterior," Julien retorted. "What about work, Pierre? What about going to work?"

"I can call in sick."

"You won't have a job if you keep doing that."

Pierre shrank back even more, his hair standing out around his face like a dirty old broom. "I'll be okay. Don't need you hovering around me."

Julien sat with his hands on the steering wheel. "No, you don't need me hovering and I don't re-member signing up to be your keeper. So that makes both of us in a bad mood."

"Bible says you are your brother's keeper."

"No, I think the verse you're referring to is Cain asking God, "Am I my brother's keeper?" Julien cranked the truck. "Which I am not."

Pierre rolled his eyes. "Yeah, and there's some-thing in there about smiting you, I'm pretty sure."

"You don't get to quote the Bible to me, bro," Julien said, his voice rising. "You don't have that right when you act like an imbecile."

"I'll quote whatever I want."

There was no reasoning with the boy, Julien decided. "I'm not taking you home. And since you're in no condition to be using a welding torch, you will call work and tell them I had an emergency and needed you with me, understand? You're going to work off the cash I just paid for your bail. And then you're gonna work off the high insurance rates and fines you will surely be paying and any lawyer or court fees I'll have to pay."

Pierre sat up, glaring over at Julien. "I am not spending the day shackled to you. I want to go home and go to bed. My head hurts."

"You are not going home to upset our mama. And your head hurts because you drank too much and now you're dehydrated."

"So, I need something else to drink."

"Water. You get water. That is it."

"Where are you taking me?"

"Shrimping," Julien replied. "Fresh air, cool breeze and no booze."

His brother grunted low while his dark eyes went wide. "You know I get seasick out in the Gulf."

"Yes, I do at that."

Julien hadn't come into the café this morning. Nor at lunch. He usually showed up by lunch at least.

Alma touched a hand to the iris Julien had sent her a few days ago. She needed to plant the thing before it died. The irony of that notion wasn't lost on Alma. When she considered putting the beautiful bulb in the ground, she saw it as a symbolic acceptance of putting down roots. And as an acceptance of allowing Julien back into her life.

Or maybe it was a sign that she could turn into a blooming idiot if she fell for him all over again.

Who was she kidding? She had already fallen for him all over again. She'd never stopped falling for him. Julien was definitely back in her life in a big way.

If she hadn't ruined things. What if this time she'd finally done the man in?

"Yu as l'air triste, chère amie."

Alma glanced over at Winnie. Her friend had a knowing smile on her round face. "I'm not sad. I'm frustrated."

"What's wrong?" Winnie asked, glancing at the flower. "Is your plant dying?"

"No, but Julien is angry with me."

Winnie's smile parted her lips. "Since when has that man not been mad at you, or about you?"

"Do you think I'm shallow and selfish, Winnie?"

Winnie glanced around as if she was being put to a test. "Not that I can see. You're generous with all of us, letting us off when we need off, closing things down so we can spend some of the holidays, especially Christmas, with our families. You have a good spirit, Alma."

"I don't mean that kind of generous," Alma replied. "I mean, do you think it's shallow of me to want…more?"

"Depends on what kind of more you want," Winnie said. Then she grabbed the order-up and took it to the family waiting in a corner booth.

Alma watched the little family while Winnie chatted and smiled at them. Tourists with two small children. Chocolate milk and pancakes for the older child. Dry cereal for the toddler. So sweet, so precious. A family. Would she ever have that?

And why hadn't Winnie explained what she meant by that last comment. What kind of *more* did Alma want?

She wanted the kind that gave her a family and children and dry cereal and chocolate milk for breakfast. She wanted the kind that let her plant irises that would grow and multiply and fill her garden with beauty and…roots.

"Figured it out yet?" Winnie asked as she slid by.

"I think maybe I have," Alma replied. "Only I think it's too late."

It was late afternoon before Julien came back into town. He'd dumped his brother back home and dared him to leave the house. Of course, their mother had stewed and fussed, immediately making Pierre a nice hot cup of ginger tea to settle his poor little ailing stomach. Then she'd reamed the boy out, telling him he needed to get his head back on straight and what would his papa think and why did he do these things to her?

And me? Julien wondered. Why did his once-normal little brother have to go all rebel on him now?

He slowed the truck near the Fleur Café.

He aimed to keep going past, to head to his warehouse and work on one of his boats. He craved a bit of solitude. But his old pickup seemed to have a mind of its own and parked right out front.

So Julien was forced to either sit there staring in or open the door and go in for a good strong cup of coffee. And something besides Vienna sausage straight from the can to eat.

He got out of the truck, stretching out the kinks he'd held so tightly while shrimping with his goose of a brother all morning. They'd hauled in a pretty good catch, which was now iced down and waiting to be distributed to various clients and friends.

He'd bring back Alma's order later.

Right now, he didn't want to think about shrimp.

He'd cleaned up and smelled better than a shrimp, at least.

So he walked into the near-empty café, glad it was past the busy lunch hour. The quiet darkness of the paneled walls cooled him down and the muted sound of zydeco music soothed him. Julien relaxed his brow for the first time today.

Pretty Mollie came traipsing out and met him at the bar. "Hello. What can I get for you?"

"Coffee and Alma," he said, not caring that the girl's eyes widened.

"I'll bring back both," she said, her smile soft and measured. Then she turned at the coffee machine. "What's up with Pierre? He didn't make it to our Bible study last night."

Bible study? Should Julien tell her his brother had been studying bottles and not Bibles lately?

"He got called away unexpectedly," Julien replied, sending up a tiny prayer for telling a tall tale.

"I'd hoped he'd come by for breakfast," Mollie continued as she placed the steaming coffee in front of Julien.

"He was tied up this morning."

Not so very far from the truth. Shackled was more like it. Shackled and then released and… the boy had spent the rest of the morning with his head bent over the side of the trawler. Tortured into getting sober.

And Pierre deserved it, for sure.

"I'll go get Alma," Mollie said on a disappointed note.

He really should warn that nice girl away from his not-so-good brother, Julien decided. But there was still good somewhere inside Pierre. He just had to drag it out. Maybe Pretty Mollie would be a good influence.

"Hello."

He looked up from nursing his coffee to find Alma standing at the end of the counter. She had on a short, flowing skirt and a muted lavender T-shirt. And another pair of those cute sneakers she liked to collect. These were hot pink and painted with yellow and blue butterflies. Colorful, but not as nervous as the butterflies fluttering to beat the band inside his stomach.

"Hi," he said. Then he looked down at his coffee.

She advanced a few steps. "Do you want a piece of pie?"

"What kind?"

"We have strawberry, chocolate and peach cobbler today."

Peach cobbler sounded good. His growling stomach agreed.

"Julien, have you had lunch?"

He shook his head. "I was out shrimping."

"I'll bring you some étouffée."

"And peach cobbler," he added. "With ice cream."

"I'll be right back."

He watched her prance away, the scent of flowers from her perfume merging with the scents of fried fish and bread baking.

His stomach called out again. Julien patted it. "Hush up."

Alma came back with the etouffée. The bowl was full of fluffy white rice covered with a creamy, reddish-orange roux mixed with onions, peppers, celery and meaty crawfish tails.

Julien stared down at the bowl, grabbed the crusty piece of bread beside it and dipped the bread into the roux. Then he took a bite, closed his eyes and savored the flavors of garlic and bay leaf mixed with all that luscious roux and vegetables. And the chewy crawfish. He nabbed a couple of bits of the tiny crustaceans on the next bite.

"You should mass produce this and sell it to all the world."

"You must have been really hungry."

He opened his eyes to find Alma staring at him. He stared back. "I was."

She stood there holding the counter like it was

the railing of a sinking ship. "I'm sorry about last night."

He took a drink of the water she'd poured for him then chased it with the coffee. "Last night? Last night? That seems like a lifetime ago."

"You're mad at me," she replied, hurt in her eyes. "I don't want you to be mad, Julien."

He put down his spoon. "*Non,* not you, *catin.*" What could he say? "It's just been a not-so-good day."

"But…it started last night, with us."

He almost reached for her hand. But he held back, gripping the white coffee cup instead. "*Non, non.* Last night, in spite of me storming off like a mad dog, was…beautiful. I had a nice time talking to you, in your home."

Her eyes widened. "You've never been inside my house before, have you?"

"No."

That little word settled and shifted on the air between them. And summed up things pretty nicely.

He ventured back toward the deep waters of his longing. "I liked being there. And I shouldn't have pushed you with all this crazy talk."

She looked surprised and maybe a tad disappointed. But her smile belied that. "So we're good again?"

His heart hurt, hearing that loaded question. "We're better than good."

"Finish up your étouffée and I'll go get your cobbler."

He did as she said, taking his bread to swipe the gravy off the bowl. Man, he'd been so hungry.

Alma came back with a big bowl of steaming peach cobbler, the flaky crust mixing with the juicy peaches. A glob of creamy vanilla ice cream slid around over the peaches.

"That smells so good," he said, taking in the nutmeg and cinnamon. "You're spoiling me."

"You're smiling now," she said, her elbows propped on the old counter. "What was wrong when you came in before?"

"Did it show so much?"

"Yes. I was worried that you were angry with me forever."

"I told you, I'm not mad at you. I'm mad because things are so messed up, you know?"

She tilted her head, one bouncy curl going along for the ride. "I know."

Julien didn't like to air his dirty laundry, but Alma would understand. "Pierre got arrested last night for driving drunk."

"Oh, no." Her hand went to her mouth. "I'm so sorry. Is he still in jail?"

"No. He's out but he's still in a peck of trouble. And it'll cost us. I'll have to find some extra cash somewhere." He hated telling her that, but Alma knew about hard times.

"Pierre was in jail? What happened?" They both looked up to see Mollie standing there, her brown eyes big and full of concern. When Julien didn't give her a quick answer, she said, "I guess that's why he missed Bible study."

Chapter Eleven

Alma looked from Julien to Mollie. "Mollie, I'm glad you're concerned about Pierre, but we don't repeat such things around here, okay? No need to spread rumors. Miss Virginia would be hurt by that."

Mollie walked up to them and then glanced around. The restaurant was mostly empty. "I'd never do that, Alma. I want to help Pierre. He's funny and cute, but he seems so sad at times. I just want him to find the love of the Lord again."

Julien shot Alma a tormented look then turned to Mollie. "How long have you known Pierre?"

"I knew him in school," the girl explained. "He was a few years ahead of me but I've always liked him."

"How old are you?" Julien asked, concern replacing the torment in his expression.

"I'm eighteen," the girl said with a soft smile. "I've waited long enough. I'm legal now."

Julien grimaced and stared at Alma. "Legal don't make it good, suga'. My brother has certain…issues."

"I know all about his issues," Mollie retorted. "That's why I want him to come to church with me." She leaned close, her brown eyes centered on Julien. "He drinks too much because he's still missing your daddy, Julien."

Alma watched as Julien's expression changed. The brightness she'd always loved in his eyes seemed to dim and go out. "*C'est vrai*, we all do."

Mollie nodded. "I'm not trying to get in your business, but Pierre's been kind of forgotten. I mean, nobody much bothers to see how he's feeling. I think spring reminds him of all the things y'all used to do with your daddy and he said your daddy's birthday is coming up. He told me it'll be a year in September since your father passed, but he said nobody ever talks about that." She brushed a hand across the counter.

Julien sat up straight. "I talk to the kid all the time."

Alma shot him a warning look. Didn't he understand what Mollie was saying? "Do you talk *to* him?" she asked in a gentle tone. "Or do you talk *at* him?"

Julien's dark eyes widened, then he squinted them shut. "*At* him, mostly. Only because he needs somebody to talk at him. He's making bad decisions."

Mollie heard Winnie calling her. Backing toward the kitchen, she said, "I've been talking *to* him and letting him talk back to me. No disrespect, but there's a big difference."

Julien grunted. "Well, yeah, but then you're Pretty Mollie and I'm just Mean Old Big Brother."

Alma hid the soft smile cresting on her face. Mollie was nothing if not blunt. But the girl had good intentions. Only, Julien was too close to the situation to listen. And too hurt right now.

Julien played with his melting ice cream. "I guess that little girl is wise beyond her years."

"She's a woman with a big crush. Not so wise, just hopeful."

He relaxed and shook his head. "Did you use to feel like that about me? You know, talking to me and listening to me when I was so bullheaded. Did I ever listen back?"

Alma leaned over the counter. "We used to talk a lot, about a lot of things. I don't know if you were always listening, but you always seemed to understand me back then. We used to talk for hours." She wondered if they'd ever reach that kind of intimacy again.

"Same here," he said, lowering his head. "You always knew the right thing to say or the right way to handle my moods." Then he reached out toward her hand, his fingers just barely touching hers. "All those others, Alma. They…we didn't talk about anything much."

She moved her fingers away. "Maybe you were too busy doing other things."

He grabbed her hand back. "I was usually thinking about you, wondering if you were with somebody else. Just thinking that made me crazy."

She didn't pull away this time. "I don't believe that for one minute. You've managed, Julien. You didn't seem the least bit bothered by me."

His eyes went dark with torment. "But have you dated other people? Have you been close to other men?"

"I've gone on a few dates here and there," she said, bad memories clouding over the comic reality of blind dates and weird setups. "Nobody special."

"Same here," he said. "And I mean that. I wanted to find someone else, so I could forget you. But nobody compared."

"Well, you've always been popular with the ladies."

"Not so much. They all figured things out."

Alma wouldn't lash out at him. It wasn't her business who he saw or dated or danced with or… kissed. But her heart beat into a jealous rage that shot her pulse straight up. She shouldn't be jealous since she'd pushed him away all those years ago. But she couldn't deny seeing him with other women had hurt.

"Maybe you shouldn't wait around for me,"

she said. "I'm so mixed up and confused, I don't know what I want anymore."

He looked down at his hand over hers. "I've always known exactly what I wanted. It's the getting it that's killing me."

Alma didn't know how to respond to that. "Eat your cobbler, Julien. It's gonna be okay. You know I will pray for your brother and you. God will see you through."

"I love God and I appreciate the prayers," he replied, letting go of her hand. "But...while you're praying, will you please ask Him to give you strength, too?"

She drew back. "Me? Strength for what?"

"Dealing with me," he said. Then he shoved the last of his cobbler in his mouth, finished it off, stood up and leaned over to give her a quick peck on the cheek. "Thanks for the nourishment."

Before she could say "You're welcome" he was out the door.

But the warmth of his lips on her cheek remained long after he'd left. As did the promise that he wasn't going to give up on her.

Alma glanced over at the potted iris. And saw a fresh new bluish-purple bud pushing up out of the green sprouts.

Julien made his deliveries for the day then headed to the boat shed, intent on getting some work done there. His time alone creating boats gave him the solitude he craved and the quiet he needed to think and reflect. And maybe pray. He needed that solitude today because he had a lot on his mind.

He pulled into the oyster-shell yard of the old warehouse near the marina, glad to be done with explaining himself for one day. Once inside, he called his mother to check on Pierre.

"Sleeping like a baby," Virginia said, relief skimming over the worry in her voice. "I've been praying for that boy all day long."

"Keep praying, Maman," Julien said. "Pray that I don't toss him out on his head next time he pulls a stunt like this."

"I can't afford a lawyer, Julien."

"I know that. Don't worry. I'll figure something out."

"You are so good to your poor mama. Will you be here for supper?"

"Probably." He told his mother goodbye then stood taking in the cool darkness of the boat shed. Even with the big doors thrown open, it wasn't nearly as hot in here as it was outside.

Julien turned on the overhead lights and the oscillating fan, the whirl of the old fan as soothing as the ocean's tide.

Studying the curve of the skeletal beginnings of the skiff, he thought it was right here a few weeks ago that he'd had the first epiphany about his life. His daddy used to say he was closer to God in a boat, out on the water.

Julien had felt close to God that night, building his boats. The quiet of this big, dusty place, the whirl of the fan and the nature of the tasks he needed to perform had all contributed to him going into a relaxed state of mind. He'd been content, open to the possibilities of life. Intent on his work, he went searching in a toolbox for an extra wood clamp and some more shank nails. He'd run across an old, yellowed picture of Pierre and him when they were little boys, fishing off a pier with their papa.

Then an image of his daddy had popped into his head. Edward LeBlanc sitting in a boat, laughing, sipping on sweet tea, eating Vienna sausage with crackers and telling tall tales. Waiting, always waiting for that next big catch.

His daddy had lived to fish and hunt alligators. And he'd died doing exactly that. But he's also died knowing he had a family that loved him. The picture Julien had found proved that.

That night, Julien had stood here in the muted yellow light from the overhead fixture and realized he was all alone. Once his mama was gone, he'd only have Pierre. If Pierre married and moved on, Julien would be left completely alone.

He'd thought of Alma, wishing he could just

sweep her up and make her his again. Wishing he hadn't been so stubborn and full of pride when he was young and full of himself.

He accepted that night there in the dusk of day that he wanted Alma back. So he prayed, really prayed, for God to show him how to win her. Julien knew God didn't just dole out solutions on demand, but he also knew that through God he might find the strength he needed to be a better man. For Alma. And for the Lord.

The signs had popped up after seeing that picture. He'd seen his mama the next day, playing with a baby. Then his mama had voiced her need for grandchildren the very next morning, the same exact morning he'd later seen Alma standing in the middle of her sweet café.

Alone.

No need for them to be apart and alone.

Better to be together and happy.

Is that the plan then, Lord?

He prayed he'd heard God right in all the signs and signals. He'd prayed before that the Lord would teach him restraint and self-control. Now his need to bring attention to himself by flirting and bar-hopping had changed to the need to make Alma see what he'd seen that morning, looking in on her.

But how could he make her see that they didn't

need to be alone anymore? That they were meant to be together.

Hammering the battens into the curved wood he'd already glued to the bow stems, Julien strained to make sure they fit inside the arch. Then he clamped the curved sides of what would become the boat to force them into a natural V-shaped fit. He was just about to start gluing and nailing when he heard footsteps.

Julien held tight to one of the clamps, but glanced up to see his brother strolling into the boat shed. "I thought you were asleep."

"I woke up," Pierre said. He automatically came over to help hold the big metal clamp on the wood. "Is this cypress?"

"Nope. Fir. Cypress is hard to come by, but I get some from South America every now and then. Of course, the old timers still like to use pure Louisiana cypress."

"Papa always said cypress makes the best boats."

Remembering what Mollie had told him, Julien decided he wouldn't fuss at his brother tonight. He wanted to help Pierre, truly he did. Maybe he'd been going about it all the wrong way.

"How you feeling?" he asked, trying to sound nonchalant.

"Considering you took me out into deep water

and watched me while I was at death's door, I wonder if you care how I'm feeling."

"You weren't at death's door," Julien said, a slight grin forming on his face. "But you sure did look as green as seaweed."

"You think that's funny?" Pierre asked, moving around to clamp the other side of the hull. He tried to hide his own grin.

"It was funny this morning," Julien replied. He almost said the rest of it wasn't so funny. But he didn't. "I'll find you a lawyer."

"Am I going to jail?"

"I don't know. We can only hope you'll get probation and a fine since it was your first offense. But you do understand this is serious, don't you?"

Pierre nodded. "I'm sorry. I had too much to drink."

"I don't want you to get hurt or, worse, kill yourself or someone else," Julien said. The same words he'd voiced that morning, but this time he used a gentle tone. "And I'm sorry I was so mad this morning."

"I know. Mama was all upset. I guess I messed up big-time."

Julien finished clamping and looked up at his brother. "Do you miss Papa?"

Pierre frowned then stared down at his big feet. "*Oui.* Don't you?"

"Every day." Julien went to the old counter and

found the picture of them. "Why don't you take this? Put it in your wallet. Think about this whenever you want to drink again."

Pierre stared at the faded, crinkled, black and white photo. "I remember this day. We caught bream and crappie, even a couple of bass. That was a good day."

Julien hated the husky tremor in his brother's voice. "We had a lot of good days. It's been more than six months now."

"Yep." Pierre touched a finger to the picture. "Summer's gonna be hard without him. Busy season. His birthday season. He said he was born in the spring so he could blossom right along with the flowers."

"He did blossom," Julien replied. "He loved being busy and working hard for his family. He depended on us to help out."

"Are you saying I'm not dependable?"

"No. I'm saying that's just the way we were raised. Our parents taught us right from wrong, but we can't expect them to watch over us all the time. Even from heaven."

"Do you think he's watching over us?"

Julien wrestled with the thoughts forming inside his head. "I think he is, *oui*. He's with God. And I'm sure they're both disappointed in the LeBlanc brothers at times. But hey, they still love us." He swallowed, looked out into the night. "And I love you, bro."

Pierre looked up at him then. "I really did it this time, didn't I?"

Julien nodded. "I've done some stupid things myself. But we're family, remember? I'll help you."

"I don't want to go to jail and I don't want to hurt anyone."

Julien came around the hull and slapped a hand on his brother's back. "Then you're gonna have to stay out of trouble, understand?"

Pierre bobbed his head. "Guess I'll go to Bible study instead of to the Backwater."

"That'll sure make Pretty Mollie happy. She was asking about you this afternoon."

"You didn't tell her—"

"I didn't tell her but she heard me mention it to Alma."

"You told Alma?"

"It's all right. She won't say a word to anyone and neither will Mollie."

"Mollie won't go out with me now, for sure."

"Oh, I think she will, but you need to tell her all about this yourself. I do believe that girl cares about you. And it only took her about what, three days, to fall for all that LeBlanc charm."

Pierre smiled for the first time that day. "She is

pretty and sweet and she has a strong faith. That should keep me on the straight and narrow."

"Does that scare you?"

"A little. I mean, I'm not exactly church material."

"None of us are church material, bro," Julien replied. "That's why they keep building churches."

"You think Mollie will be mad about what I did?"

"Not if you're honest with her. And not if you try hard to do right."

It occurred to Julien that he ought to take his own advice. He'd never really told Alma all the reasons he'd acted so crazy the night of the prom. Maybe it was time for him to be honest, too. He'd tried and he'd given her hints, but if he wanted a future with her, he needed to be completely truthful with her.

"I'll try to do better," Pierre said, his words a soft echo against the whirl of the old fan.

"That's all I can ask," Julien replied.

The brothers worked together in a comfortable silence for a while longer, gluing and nailing wood into parts that became a boat while they mended their relationship with the glue and nails of a faith that made them family.

But while Pierre battled his own inner turmoil, Julien met his challenges head-on. He planned to

make Alma his again. She was coming around
and that was nice, but he would take his time
and show her that he'd changed, that he could be
enough for her. He'd provide for her and show her
how much he loved her so she'd never miss that
big old world out there.

And he'd do it with God's help and lots of
prayers. And with more talking-to instead of talk-
ing-at.

Chapter Twelve

"Elvis, go away!"

Alma pushed at the big mutt her sister Callie had taken in after her husband had left. Elvis had started out as a cute abandoned puppy, a black-and-white bundle of energy. Four years later, he was now a big, drooling chunk of dog, a bit of Catahoula hound mixed with what might have been a Great Dane. No one was sure. But he was as awkward and clumsy as a runaway johnboat, always whirling and hopping and grunting out little mock barks, his blue-tinged eyes anxious to play. Elvis made things around Callie's Corner Nursery interesting and amusing.

He backed up to sit and hit a pot centered on a wrought-iron plant stand. The pot went sailing off the short-legged stand and crashed into three pieces.

"Callie, please put Elvis out back," Alma called.

"I can't concentrate on finding plants to use on the festival tables with this big mutt following me around."

Callie hurried over, shaking her head at the broken pot. "Elvis, you promised you'd behave if I let you into the front of the shop."

"He has broken that promise and a very nice flowerpot, too," Alma retorted. She shot Elvis an accusing glance.

The big, shaggy dog flopped down and stared up at her with doleful, silvery eyes. Alma felt badly for reprimanding him, so she leaned down and rubbed his big head. "Sorry."

"C'mon, old boy," Callie said.

The big dog stood and hurried after Callie but stopped with a flat-footed skid when he realized he was about to be put in time-out inside the dog run at the back of the big nursery lot.

"Don't give me that sad look," Callie said. "We'll go for a long walk later, I promise."

Alma smiled at her sister's chatter. That dog, clumsy and ox-like, had brought her sister countless hours of pleasure and companionship. And love. The dog had shown up at exactly the right moment when Callie was at a low point in her life. Callie loved Elvis in spite of all his obvious flaws.

Julien came to mind. Did Alma want to love

him again in spite of his flaws? Had he shown up back in her life at exactly the right moment?

"Staring at that geranium won't make it bloom any faster," Callie said from behind Alma.

She whirled and, like Elvis, almost knocked over a plant. "You scared me, sneaking up on me like that."

"I wasn't being sneaky," Callie replied. "Just minding my own business in my own place of business." She poked Alma in the ribs with her elbow. "Rumor has it that you and Julien have been spending a lot of time together."

Alma bristled. "You shouldn't listen to rumors."

"Is it true?"

"Well, the man eats at the café a lot. And we are on the festival committee together."

Callie grinned at that. "Yeah, according to Tebow's mom, Julien only comes to the meetings to stare at you. Seems he was really taken with your dobash cake."

"Miss Frances is just imagining things, I reckon," Alma replied. "She's too busy staring at our daddy during those meetings to notice anyone else. And if I recall, she seemed to enjoy that cake, too."

"Love all around me," Callie said, her sigh long-suffering. "I guess I'll stick to Elvis. I can at least trust him to stay around when the going gets tough."

Alma silently chastised herself for even complaining. Callie deserved to be loved, had poured her heart into her short-lived marriage. But Bobby Moreau hadn't had the fortitude to handle her illness. The man had drifted away the minute Callie had learned she had breast cancer, and even though he'd been around while she accepted and fought her illness, he'd never actually dealt with things or given her the kind of support she'd needed, even after she'd gone through chemo and radiation. He left the day the doctor gave Callie the news that she was in full remission. Left his beautiful, heart-broken, weary wife because he couldn't deal with something he couldn't control.

No wonder Callie loved Elvis.

"So what kind of flowers do you want for the tables?" Callie asked now, her hands on her hips, her hair up in a tumbled, caramel-colored bun.

"I don't know." Alma trailed her fingers over the Gerbera daisies and lush geraniums. "The tables will be under the big festival tent. So what do you suggest?"

Callie glanced around. "Remind me again what the theme is this year?"

"New Beginnings," Alma said, wondering why the joke was on her. "You know, after the storms, after the oil spill, after the long winter. After—"

"A new beginning after ignoring the man you've loved for almost ten years?" Callie said, her smile soft and knowing. "It's okay to talk about it with me, Alma. I can handle it. I'm a big girl."

"I'm sorry," Alma said. She reached for a small pot of Mexican heather. "I don't know how I feel myself but I don't want to rub it in with you, either."

Callie halted her with a hand on her arm. "So you're not going to go after love and happiness just because your older sister got jilted after surviving cancer?"

"It's not fair," Alma said. "None of this is fair."

"We all know that old saying 'the fair only comes once a year and that's in the fall.'"

"I hate seeing you so hurt."

Callie leaned back against one of the plant tables. "I was hurt, true. And it wasn't fair. But Alma, you can't stop living just because I had a bad run. Bobby wasn't ready for all that I had to go through. Sometimes I think he loved me too much. Too much to handle anything but what he thought was a perfect marriage."

"I hate perfect," Alma stated, deciding she liked the Mexican heather. "Perfect demands too much, asks too much."

"None of us are perfect," Callie said, taking the flat of heather Alma shoved at her. "I take it you want me to replant these into cute little pots for your tables?"

Alma bobbed her head. "I know I'm certainly not perfect, so why do I judge Julien so harshly? Why do I push him away even when I want him nearby? When I dream about his kisses and his kindness and—" She headed toward the daisies and lifted a flat of bright yellow and orange blooming clusters. "These would be nice, too."

"Got it," Callie said, motioning for a nearby sales clerk to come and help her.

Alma didn't notice her sister struggling with the load of flats. "We don't have it all figured out, Callie. We're both a mess, because of cancer, because of missing our mother, because of your divorce. We're seriously messed up. I'm so glad Brenna's happy at least."

Callie looked away then scratched her head.

Which cause Alma to stop and stare at her. "Brenna is happy, isn't she?"

Callie didn't answer.

"Callie, what aren't you telling me?"

"She called me last night. In tears. They had another fight."

Alma's heart felt like a lead weight inside her chest. "Is there going to be a wedding this summer?"

"I don't know," Callie said with a shrug. "I'm not so sure anymore. But you know Brenna. She's always a bit dramatic about things. I hope they'll work it out. They always do."

Alma wasn't so sure either. "But what if one of these fights turns into the real thing and Brenna doesn't get her big wedding after all?"

Callie leaned close then reached for a batch of bright pink dahlias. "Then I guess our sister will do what we've been doing all this time. She'll survive."

Julien didn't think he could survive until the weekend. He wanted to go out on a real date with Alma. So he looked into the glass door of the Fleur Café and saw her behind the counter, same as just about every other day in his life since they'd both graduated from high school.

Why had he waited so long to win her back? What if he'd waited too late?

She looked up and saw him and smiled. That was a good sign.

Julien opened the door and walked in, smiling back. "Good morning."

"Hi." She motioned to a bar stool. "Want some coffee?"

"Yes," Julien said, waiting for the other shoe to drop.

"Where's Tebow been?" She poured him a cup right from the fresh pot. Not the already-been-sitting-there-for-hours pot, but the freshly made coffee pot.

Another good sign.

"Tebow's been in New Orleans visiting a woman, I believe. But he's also actually working. You know he does construction on the side for some hotshot millionaire who likes to invest in restoration projects."

"We all have jobs on the side, don't we?" she asked with another sweet smile.

Julien felt the hairs on the back of his neck standing up. What was his Alma up to this morning, with all the sweetness and light?

"You okay?" he asked before taking a cautious sip of the steaming black coffee.

"I'm fine," Alma said, bringing him the entire tray of freshly baked muffins and croissants. "Want some mayhew jelly with one of these?"

"Make it two croissants and a plate of eggs," Julien said, going with the moment but wishing he had Tebow here to test the food.

He waited, holding his breath, while Alma breezed around barking polite little orders and greeting customers. What was going on? Since when did she treat him nicely?

Well, she'd always been civil and polite. But nice? That was a whole different thing. She'd been nice the other day after lunch when he'd told her about Pierre, too. He'd appreciated it that day and he appreciated it now. Only, it was different and a tad scary.

He started praying, a silent little plea for the Lord to show him the way to handle a nice Alma.

"Here's your food," she said, startling him out of his fervent prayers. "How are you, anyway?"

"Me, I'm good. Good." He leaned back to stare at the food.

"Something wrong?"

"No, nothing. Looks great." He took a tentative bite of the fluffy eggs. "Hmm. Good. Real good."

"How's Pierre?" she asked, her blue eyes going soft.

So was she being nice because she felt pity toward him and his little brother? Or was she being nice because she really felt something for him and she wanted to turn things up a notch?

Not knowing what to say, Julien focused on her question about his brother. "He's better. He's at work. Made it just about the whole week this week. His hearing is set for next Monday, so we'll see how the judge decides."

"Well, that's something, then." She patted his hand then turned back toward the kitchen. "I'll be back to check on you in a minute or two."

Not *I'll see you later, Julien* but *I'll be back to check on you.*

This was a vast improvement. Maybe he was winning her over after all. Her actions and his four cups of strong coffee gave him a buzz of encouragement. So while Alma went about her busy work, Julien smiled and chatted with both locals and tourists alike. He charmed Sweet Mollie and teased her about reforming his bad little brother. He winked at Frances Laborde and asked after her health, giving her sympathetic nods when she mentioned her gout was acting up. And he didn't even flinch when Ramon Blanchard stomped into the café like a bull charging toward a red flag.

Julien did a spin on his bar stool. "Morning, Mr. Blanchard!"

"Hmph. Dat depends on a lot of things, one of them being you," Ramon retorted before going to greet another businessman.

The fact that Alma's formidable papa hadn't taken him by the neck and tried to squeeze the life out of him gave Julien even more courage and hope. This was turning out to be a rather great morning.

Finally, the breakfast crowd cleared out and Alma came back with yet another fresh pot of coffee to give Julien his sixth refill. "One more for the road?" she asked.

Okay, so maybe she was tired of him sitting here watching her. "Uh, yeah, sure. Hey, Alma. I wanted to ask you something."

She stopped, coffeepot in hand, her eyes as dark blue as the iris that was blooming on the counter. The iris he'd given her to plant in her yard. To remind her of him.

"Uh-huh?"

He swallowed, glanced around to make sure her papa wasn't listening. "I thought maybe we could have dinner together Friday night. Maybe in New Orleans?"

Alma set down the coffeepot. "Dinner? In New Orleans? You and me? Friday night?"

"Yeah, you and me. In New Orleans. You know, take a long ride, have someone wait on you and serve you a good meal for a change?"

She played with her heart-shaped gold necklace. "Friday's my busy night."

He pushed at a Tabasco bottle. "Every night is your busy night."

"But Friday is my busiest night."

His heart turned as sour as all the coffee in his stomach. "So, you're saying no?"

"No, I'm not saying that." She looked embarrassed. "I'll be right back."

Julien watched, sweat gathering in a big drop and snaking down his spine, as she pulled Winnie aside and whispered something in her ear.

Winnie looked at him, grinned, then bobbed her head. Alma turned and trotted on her cute blue tennis shoes back to Julien.

"Yes, I'll go out to dinner with you, in New Orleans, on Friday night."

Julien turned his head from side to side. "Did I hear that right?"

She smiled again. "Yes, Julien. You heard that right. I might be crazy, but I'd enjoy a night out. It's been a long time since—"

"Since anyone has taken care of you?"

Her smile trembled a little bit. "Yes."

"I'll pick you up around six-thirty so we can get there early and stay late. I haven't been into New Orleans in a while myself."

Her smile was shy but steady. "All right. I'll see you then."

Julien paid his tab, left a hefty tip, smiled at Ramon Blanchard and then headed for the door. He couldn't help but whistle a happy tune. Alma was going out with him Friday night. Two more whole days before he could get her away from her sister, her father and all the prying eyes in this town. Two more days until he could really have a nice, intimate talk with her and take her for a moonlit stroll in one of the most romantic cities in the world.

Yep, his morning had turned out very good. He had a date with Alma, finally.

He only hoped nothing bad happened between now and then.

Chapter Thirteen

They were on their way over the Fleur Bay Bridge when Alma's cell phone rang.

"I'm sorry," she said, glancing over at Julien. Her heart was still fluttering about the way he'd cleaned up. He looked good in a crisp, short-sleeved, button-up white shirt that set off his tan and pressed navy pants that she was pretty sure he only wore to church and funerals.

"Hello?"

"Where are you?"

"Brenna?"

Her sister burst into a wail. "Yes."

Julien shot her a concerned glance. Alma held up a hand to him, mouthed *my sister* and then listened into the phone while she clutched her light-weight cream wrap with her other hand. "What's wrong?"

"I just needed to hear your voice," Brenna said. "Jeffrey and I had another fight."

"Besides the one you called Callie about?"

Julien pulled the old truck off the road into a small park after they'd made it across the long bridge. "I'll wait here," he whispered. Then he got out of the truck, probably to give Alma some privacy.

Alma tugged at the teal sleeveless dress she was wearing, her body suddenly chilled by her younger sister's obvious despair. "Are you all right?"

"No," Brenna said, sniffing. "I'm a basket case. I don't normally burst into tears like this but I just don't know if we'll work through this."

"What's the problem?" Alma asked, her gaze moving over Julien standing there in the growing sunset. She really wanted to go on this date to test the waters between them. As usual, her sister's timing wasn't so good.

"It's my family—us—me," Brenna replied. "Jeff thinks we're all backwater rednecks."

"Well, honey, we kind of are."

"But he's rude about it. When I was talking about the wedding and the guest list, he made a disparaging comment about too many pickups and boats pulling up to the church."

Alma had to smile at that. Jeffrey had probably come close to the truth, but the man was a helpless snob from old Baton Rouge money and that had been a bone of contention between Brenna and her soon-to-be husband since the beginning. "Oh, we'd leave the boats down on the Mississippi," she retorted. "But we might ride up on a big ol' alligator or two."

"It's not funny, Alma."

"No, it's not," she said, sending an apologetic wave to Julien. The man was patiently staring out at the big bay that sprawled between Fleur and some of the barrier islands along the coast. "So y'all had an argument based on that."

"Based on a lot of things," Brenna said. "He doesn't want my family involved in anything. He's barely tolerating you and Callie as my bridesmaids. He wanted his snobby old sister to be my maid of honor. I don't even like her."

"But you'll need to get along with her if you marry into the family. Maybe she could be a bridesmaid with us."

"I can deal with the woman, just not standing by me when I get married. I won't have Papa paying triple for the kind of designer features she'd demand in my wedding. I want to keep the overhead simple and inexpensive, and I want you and Callie there with me, along with a couple of my sorority sisters, of course."

"Of course." Alma thought Brenna had picked up on some of that snobbishness, but her sister tried to walk between two worlds—her old simple-folk one in Fleur and her new artsy-wealthy one in Baton Rouge. "Bree, you know Papa only wants you to be happy. He doesn't mind the money."

"Well, I do. I know he's got money tucked back for all of us, but I won't bankrupt my own daddy just to please Jeffrey and his uppity family."

"Do you even want to marry into that kind of family?"

"I'm not so sure."

"I see," Alma said. She glanced back at Julien and saw him check his watch. "Listen, honey, I have to go. I'm on my way to New Orleans—"

"New Orleans? Why?"

Like I don't have a life, Alma thought. "Well, I'm on a date, actually."

"A date? You?"

"It happens," Alma shot back, trying to hold her bitterness inside. Brenna was a bit self-absorbed these days.

"Who is he?"

Did she dare tell her high-strung sister about Julien?

Alma took the plunge. "It's Julien. Julien LeBlanc."

"Your old boyfriend? The one you kissed?"

"Uh, yes. We've gotten close again lately so we're seeing where it goes."

"Okay, so he kissed you and now you're dating again? I can't believe that. You said you'd never forgive him. Ever. I was only fourteen, but I remember a lot about that bad breakup."

Alma winced at that statement. "Yeah, well, I've said a lot of things, but I've learned that never is a very long time."

Brenna's tone chilled a bit. "I'll let you go, then. I'm sorry I bothered you."

Now, of course, Alma felt badly that she'd interrupted her sister's rant. "Are you sure you're okay?"

"I will be. I needed you to tell me to snap out of this crying jag. This is so not me. Should I marry Jeffrey?"

Why did she always get the loaded questions, Alma wondered. "Do you love Jeffrey?"

"Yes. But I'm not so sure I like him."

"Well, you still have a few months until the wedding. You can stop the whole thing right now. But, Bree, you *do* need to snap out of this diva-having-a-tantrum routine. You're right—that is so not you." Close, but not this bad at least.

"Do I sound that awful?"

"You sound like a nervous bride. Change is never easy. Even a good change. If you don't want this wedding to happen, you need to decide now and not later. The longer you wait, the worse it will become."

"I'm thinking about it. I love Jeffrey so much, but I can't imagine having to deal with his criticism all the time. I'm better than that, Alma. I've worked hard and I love him. I've tried to compromise on a lot of things, but he won't budge on anything. What more do I have to do? I'm so confused."

"But you're sounding stronger already. You need to decide what you can deal with and what you don't want to settle for. Money and prestige are great, but not at the expense of your soul, honey."

"Okay, now I have something to chew on, as Grand-mère used to say." Brenna's whine had turned into a decisive tone.

Alma smiled into the phone. "That's what I'm here for. I'll call you tomorrow, okay?"

"Okay. Love you."

"Love you, too."

Alma hung up then motioned to Julien. He came bouncing back to the truck.

"Everything okay?"

"I'm not sure. Brenna's engaged to a rich Baton Rouge man and...they can't seem to make their different backgrounds work."

He cranked the truck. "At least we come from the same background, huh?"

"Yes. We do." She stared out the window, some of the excitement of this night sizzling out. She'd just advised her younger sister not to settle, but was she about to do that herself? "Maybe I should go up to Baton Rouge and visit with her. Callie and I went a few months ago to help her start planning the wedding and to shop for bridesmaid dresses. I know she misses Mama right now." And it would be an excuse to find some space to think.

"*Oui.* Girls like having their mama at wedding time."

Alma could relate to that and more. "All the time."

He gave her a sympathetic look. "I miss my daddy every day."

Thoughts of finding distance evaporated right out of her mind. "We have that in common, too, don't we?"

"Yes."

They were quiet for a while, the sunset chasing them, the water coming and going with each twist of the road. The truck moved over the bridges and waterways and into the city, a silver-gold glow from the last of the sun gliding down over the buildings and inlets.

"I'm glad you agreed to come," Julien said as he drove the truck down the off-ramp and into the stream of New Orleans traffic. "I hope you like the restaurant."

"Italian will be a nice change," Alma said, suddenly shy for some strange reason. "We don't have that much around Fleur."

He hit the dash when the radio died. "I just wish I had a better car for you."

"Julien, don't apologize. I love this truck."

He seemed surprised at that. "You do?"

"Of course. I love your old truck. I've always been a Chevy girl."

He found a parking place in the public lot near the Quarter and then leaned over toward her. "You used to be my Chevy girl."

"Yes." She left it at that, her heart pounding too hard to let her find a breath. This truck was that old, and she remembered many a night sitting here beside him near a body of water, talking, laughing, kissing.

Maybe this wasn't such a good idea after all.

She used to be a lot of things, but she had changed. And after hearing her sister lamenting about whether to get married or not, Alma wasn't sure if she wanted to dive back into a serious relationship after all. Too many complications.

But when Julien came around the truck and opened the door for her, the hope in his dark eyes grabbed hold of her and held her. That hope gave Alma the courage to step out of the truck and take his hand. They both needed this night away from everything.

After all, they did have that much in common.

Julien escorted Alma through the Quarter, the charm of the old buildings reminding him of all the things he loved about his home state. He shot covert glances toward Alma to see if she was enjoying their stroll toward the restaurant. She looked so pretty in that blue dress. Her hair was pulled back in some kind of curling upswept 'do that begged to be let down. He wanted to run his hands through her dark curls and tug them free.

"Have you ever eaten at Mama's Pasta and Pizza?" he asked to distract himself. He hoped this would be a new experience for her.

"No." Her smile lit up her face. "Is that where we're going?"

"Yeah. I wanted to surprise you but I couldn't wait. I also wanted to make sure you'd like going there. It's kind of off the beaten path, but well worth the long walk."

She bobbed her head. "I've heard a lot about the place. Back when I was searching for jobs outside of Fleur, I actually filled out an application to work there."

"Really?" Julien's heart did a flip-flop. What if she had gotten that job? Would he have seen her again? He stopped underneath a street lamp and held her arm while they waited for the foot traffic to die down. "Have you ever regretted staying in Fleur?"

"Yes," she said, her eyes open and honest. "I stayed when my mom got so sick and there were times when I wanted to run away. But I'm okay with that now, I think. I'm glad I stayed to be with her in her last days."

"And now?"

She looked in the window of one of the antique stores lining Royal Street. A fancy clock ticked away, its gilded face sparkling in the dusk. "And now, I like my work. I can cook up anything I want and test it out on the locals or serve it up to the unsuspecting tourists. I'm content."

Julien didn't believe her. Was he doing the right thing, pursuing her and trying to make a life with her? That had always been the overriding question in his life. "Why haven't you left? I mean, you always talked about it. Why not just do it?"

She gave him a startled little look. "I…uh…told you, I stayed because my mama got sick. Somebody had to help run the café. After a while, it seemed as if I was destined to be there. I love cooking and I love being with people. I can do that in Fleur same as anywhere else."

They were almost to the restaurant, but Julien stopped her again. "So you settled?"

Anger and shock clouded her blue eyes. "I didn't say that."

"But you did settle. You always wanted to travel, explore, work in exotic restaurants."

She gave him a long look. "I'd still like to do that one day maybe. I don't know." She shrugged. "Every now and then, I hear about openings in other restaurants and sometimes I even send in a résumé and application, thinking it's time to move on. But Julien, why are we discussing this?"

A crowd of teenagers walked by, jostling Julien right into Alma. He grabbed her arms to keep from knocking her off the sidewalk. Then he glanced down at her and saw the confusion in her eyes. "I don't want to sway you, Alma. I didn't want to hold you back then and I don't want to hold you back now."

Her anger disappeared right along with the noisy teenagers, but a dark wariness came into her eyes. "No one is holding me back, except maybe me, myself and I. So stop worrying about it." She touched a hand to his face and Julien felt the rasp of work-worn calluses on her fingers. But to him, those raw, raspy slivers felt like shreds of warm silk against his skin.

He reached up for her hand and kissed the rough places on her fingers. "Alma, I just want you to be sure this time."

She stared up at him, her eyes misty now. "*I* want to be sure, too. I want so many things. Can we please enjoy this night without anything heavy weighing us down? Just for now?"

"*Mais oui,* I think we can do that. That is why I brought you here."

She smiled then and Julien leaned his forehead

against hers. "It's so nice, being with you, seeing you relaxed and happy."

"It is nice," she said, lifting her head to stare up at him. "And I'm starving. So let's go eat."

He grinned at that. His Alma did love good food.

When they got to the nondescript entryway that consisted of two shuttered windows and an old brown door, people were already waiting to get in. "It's not very big," he explained. "Do you mind a wait?"

"No. It's a nice night."

After Julien put their name on the waiting list, they found a quiet spot near a crape myrtle tree. Julien leaned against the slender tree, causing tiny pink blossoms to rain down on them.

He smiled as Alma tried to get them out of her hair. "Leave them. They look pretty with your dress."

She stopped fidgeting and smiled over at him. "Is this as weird to you as it feels for me?"

He nodded. "Last time we were on a date—"

"You left with another girl."

He hit a hand to his head. "Yep. Stupid me."

She quit smiling. "I want to understand you, Julien. I want us to be friends again. But before we can take things any further, I need you to explain to me why you left me standing in the middle of the dance floor at the prom and why I finally found you drunk and in the arms of another woman."

"Like I said," he began, swallowing the lump of discouragement in his throat, "stupid me."

"I'll go with the stupid part, but I still need the real reason you did that," she said on a sweet smile.

In spite of the pleasant temperature outside and the pleasant temperament of the night, Julien started sweating.

Chapter Fourteen

They were called to their table before Julien had to answer. After they were seated at a bistro table by the window, complete with white tablecloth and one red rose in a bud vase, Julien waited until the frazzled waiter left with their drink orders before sitting back to stare over at Alma.

"Don't let the name of this place fool you. It's casual but the food is serious. Real serious. The best lasagna ever. Even better than my mama's."

"Hmm."

She had her nose buried in the menu. He could barely see her eyes over the rim of the tall menu book.

"See anything you like?"

She kept staring at the menu. "Not yet."

"We can go somewhere else."

She peered over the menu at him, looking like a kitten peeking through a window. "I haven't read the entrées yet."

"So you're just staring at words?"

"Yep. And waiting."

He cleared his throat. "Waiting for me to answer your question?"

"Yes. Since I've been waiting close to ten years, I guess I can wait a few more minutes."

"You're not making this easy, you know?"

"Oh, yes. I know. But it wasn't easy to see you self-destructing on prom night either."

"I thought we were going to keep things light. You said you didn't want to talk about anything heavy. Didn't we kind of go over this stuff at your place the other night anyway?"

"I know I said keep it light and yes, we skimmed the surface the other night. But we're here, away from everything and everybody. And I really just need to know before I can move forward. I mean, really, really know and understand. You can take your time and we can keep it light and easy. No conflict, no judgment. Just two people having a conversation about the past. And maybe, the future."

She finished her speech then hid behind the menu again.

He grabbed the heavy food chart and slapped it on the table. "Look at me now, Alma."

She shifted on her chair and picked up the menu again, but she did glance his way. "I'm very aware of you, Julien."

"And what do you see?"

She studied him a tad too long for his comfort. "I see an older version of the boy I saw that night. You've definitely matured physically."

"So I just look older, but not much wiser?"

"No, not older. Better. More settled and mature." Her expression softened. "But I see grief in your eyes. I see it when you don't think I'm looking. I see worry—about your mama and your brother. I do see you, Julien. And I believe you've changed."

"I have changed."

The waiter came back with their iced mint tea.

Julien touched a finger to the cold glass. "I have changed," he repeated on a low voice. "I think it started the day my daddy died. It took a while. I went on regular binges after he died, trying to get even with the world and God. I was so angry. I wanted my daddy back."

"So you acted out with women and parties and embarrassing your poor mother. But haven't you been doing that since high school?"

Sweat chilled his backbone. "Yes, I did and I have. I'm not proud of it."

"Why did you stop?"

He took a sip of tea and accepted the third-degree questioning. "That was gradual, too. I got tired of waking up with a hangover and no memory of who I'd talked to the night before."

He looked down at the table. "And I heard *Maman* crying late one night. That nearly broke my heart." He didn't tell Alma about finding the picture of him with his papa and Pierre or his mama's great need to see her grandchildren before she left this earth. That would be implying a lot more than Alma was ready to hear right now.

Alma put down the menu and leaned forward. "I've never seen my daddy cry, except at my mama's funeral. But I'm pretty sure he does cry, though, a lot. He seems to want to be alone more now than he wants to be with people."

Julien cupped his hands together. "I can understand that feeling."

She took a sip of the rich, caramel-colored tea. "So you've changed. I can agree to that. But that still doesn't answer the original question."

How could he tell her? "I panicked that night. We were dancing and talking about the future. And all I had on my mind was asking you to…to marry me."

Her intake of breath caused a few people nearby to glance around. "You were going to propose?"

"Maybe not that night, but soon after," he admitted. "It's all I could think about. I'd saved money—"

She held a hand to her mouth. "And all I could

think about or talk about was leaving Fleur, getting away from the smell of fish and the summer heat and the café. I went on and on about my future. *My future.* Not ours."

He felt a great rush of relief moving throughout his system. "I was terrified—if I asked you to marry me, you'd feel obligated and you might stay. But would you be happy? If I let you go, would you resent me and hate me forever? Or worse, forget me and never come back."

He looked across the table and watched her eyes grow misty. "I didn't know what to do, *chère.* Honestly."

"So you got drunk and did the stupid thing?"

"Yes. I guess I gave up. Just gave up, because I didn't think I was worth you having to choose. I didn't want you to have to choose. What if you chose me and I fell short or disappointed you or couldn't provide for you? I didn't have a future beyond high school, Alma. No college, no choices." He waved a hand in the air. "All I've ever known is the Gulf and those swamps and bayous out there. That's all I had to offer and we both know that's a hard life. Especially these days. So I gave up. I thought you deserved better." And truth be told, even now he thought she deserved better. But he wanted to be worthy of her. So here he sat, sweating and wishing.

"You didn't trust me enough to let me make

that decision?" she asked, back to her interrogation tone.

"I didn't want you to have to make that decision."

She stared out the window, watching as people strolled by. "Did you care about that other girl?"

"What other girl? I don't even remember her name. I was disrespectful to both of you that night."

She sat back, her hands in her lap. "I'm sorry, Julien. I never dreamed… I never considered that my actions could cause such consequences. I could have pushed the issue and made you tell me the truth, but I guess I just gave up, too."

"Don't blame yourself. It was me. I didn't trust you or myself. I wanted something that I was afraid I shouldn't have. I still feel that way, but I have changed, Alma. I have. I'm willing to fight for you this time."

Alma thought about their conversation through the antipasto and the chicken lasagna. The food was wonderful, but her heart felt heavy and scarred. Knowing how much she must have hurt Julien only added to how much she cared about him now. She'd always understood that the fundamental difference between them had been her need to see the world and his need to keep his world intact.

But she'd never realized until now that she'd hurt him as much as he'd hurt her. Alma had placed all the blame on Julien because he'd acted so out of character that night. Or maybe his true character had come into play that night. In spite of his bravado and swagger, Julien had a vulnerable spot in his heart.

She'd been warned from grammar school that the LeBlanc boys were bad news. Bayou trash, one friend used to say. Too dangerous and impulsive, another prim friend warned. Her sisters had pointed out all the bad things she needed to know about Julien, but they'd also seen the good in him and in the end, her family had grudgingly accepted him.

But no matter that—Julien had been too irresistible, too much of a temptation and a challenge, to ignore. And yet Julien had always been a gentleman with her. He'd always respected her and treated her like a princess. Maybe he should have been more honest with her. Maybe he shouldn't have put such high hopes on her. Did he think she was flawless? Without sin? Too perfect for the likes of him? That was pure silly. And misguided.

And maybe I shouldn't have been so blunt and honest with him. Maybe I shouldn't have set myself up as high and mighty and determined to leave him. That was just a dream, anyway.

She'd been living in a dream that could never

come true, a dream that included the whole scope of the world, but not Julien's world. And Julien's world should have been the one she wanted more than a life of her own, on her own.

He'd believed she wanted everything but him.

She'd believed he wanted anything but her.

And that was her fault.

Could they possibly meet somewhere in the middle?

He glanced over at her now, his tone upbeat. "Hey, want some dessert? The tiramisu is really good."

She really wasn't hungry but his expression held such expectation, she couldn't deny him dessert. "Can we share? I ate too much bread and lasagna."

"I'd be willing to share."

Alma saw the twinkle in his dark eyes. He was willing to share—his heart, his love, his dreams. The man was still irresistible. And still dangerous. But he also had a heart as big as that Gulf he loved so much. A big, deep heart that hurt with all the woes of his family and the people he cared about. Including her.

Why hadn't she seen this before?

She pushed aside all the revelations clouding her judgment. "All right. I'd love a cup of coffee, too."

He placed the order then smiled over at her, his

dark gaze washing her in a sweet need. "We managed to get through dinner in a passable fashion."

"Yes. The food was very good. Nice choice."

He pointed a finger at her. "You could show them a thing or two, though. You could always apply for a position again. Any restaurant in New Orleans would love to have you."

Was he testing her already? "I need formal education, though. You know how chefs are at fancy restaurants. Temperamental and high strung. They expect perfection."

"Yeah, I know a very cute one who seems to be that way at times."

Was that how the people around her viewed her? As some sort of perfectionist who couldn't give in to any standards but her own? "I am not. I'm very even-keeled compared to my little sister."

He grinned. "Okay, you've got a point there."

The waiter brought their dessert and they dug into the creamy ladyfingers soaked in coffee liqueur and mascarpone cheese topped with creamy whipped egg whites.

"This is good," Alma said. She took another spoonful. "I haven't made tiramisu in a long time. I'll have to try it again."

"Just keep making that dobash cake, darlin', and you'll be fine."

"So you liked the cake?"

He winked at her. "You know it."

Alma thought she didn't know anything for sure, except that being around him again made her heart do strange little tumbling hops of joy. And trepidation.

They finished dessert and Julien paid the bill. "Want to take a stroll along the river?"

"Sure. I haven't been here in a long time. I love the Moonwalk."

He guided her out of the restaurant and back up Royal Street toward the main part of the Quarter. "Looks like the streets are heavy with people tonight."

"It's a pretty night," Alma replied, well aware of his hand on her back. She shifted her wrap.

"Are you cold?"

"No, no." These chills weren't because of the mild temperature outside. More from her beating heart and the rising temperature of her attraction to him. Shivers and chills. That's how he made her feel.

They reached the area around Jackson Square and crossed Decatur just past the Café Du Monde then headed up the steps leading to the Moonwalk and the Mississippi River. Alma breathed in the scents of beignets and coffee, the fishy smell of the river and the sweet lemony essence of magnolias. She touched her hand to a lush bougainvillea vine covered in delicate fuchsia-colored blossoms.

"Look at that moon," Julien said, taking her hand in his as they strolled along the Moonwalk back toward Canal Street.

Alma could hear the river water lapping at the heavy wooden steps down to the Mississippi. Her heart seemed to be caught in the waves, shifting and moving inside her body in a rhythm that took her breath away.

Off behind them, the St. Louis Cathedral glowed like a beacon in the night and the sounds of music playing and people laughing echoed out over the Quarter.

Alma glanced up to the full moon, her hand secure in the warmth of his strong fingers. "Beautiful."

At a lamp pole near some low-hanging trees, he stopped and pulled her close. "Very beautiful."

He was looking at her and not the moon.

In another breath, he was kissing her.

Alma sighed in his arms, the night breeze teasing through her hair and flowing across her lightweight wrap. The warmth of Julien's strong body surrounded her, making her realize how much she'd missed him over the years. But she wasn't kissing a confused schoolboy now. She was kissing a full-grown man who knew what he wanted out of life.

Why couldn't she be so sure?

As if sensing her fears, Julien pulled back. "What's wrong, *chère?*"

"Nothing," she whispered. "Everything."

"We've got a long way to go, don't we?"

She nodded, unable to voice what was in her heart, the taste of their mint chocolate after-dinner candy still on her lips. The taste of his touch still warming her soul.

Julien lifted her chin with his finger. "I'm going to prove myself to you, Alma. I promise. This time, in spite of my worries, I'm not gonna do anything to mess this up. I mean that. I'll make us a life and I'll work hard to honor that pledge."

He stared down at her, a questioning look on his face. "But I need to know something."

"What?"

"Do you still have that dream of going away?"

Alma thought about that. Did she want Paris and Rome? Did she want New Orleans or Atlanta? She didn't know, honestly. Right now, she only wanted to be here in his arms.

"Julien, you're not holding me back," she whispered. "I have a responsibility to my family and that has to come first. I think I'll be in Fleur a long, long time. If I stay, it won't be because you're holding me back. It will be because I can't leave. Because I don't want to leave."

"I don't want to hold you back," he said, "but I can't let you go, either. I tried that route and it didn't work so well. If you stay, I want it to be because you want to be with me and not out there somewhere far away." He leaned in, his eyes swirling like dark chocolate. "I want you to choose me, Alma. But I want you to be sure when you do. Do you understand?"

She nodded, unable to say anything.

"Do you believe me?"

She believed him. She kissed him again to show him that she wanted to trust him. And, maybe, to show him that she didn't want to go that route again either. If only she could be completely sure.

She said a silent prayer: *Please, Lord, show us the way. Show me what to do, how to let go and love this man completely. Am I where I'm supposed to be? Is he the one, Lord?*

The way Julien looked down at her with the moonlight spilling out of his black eyes, she thought yes, he was the one. The way he kissed her made her feel whole and needed and cherished and loved. Wasn't that feeling more important than what she might be missing out beyond these waters?

Somewhere off in the distance, a lonely saxophone played a soulful, bluesy tune that seemed to match her mood. The poignant notes lifted out into the night and touched Alma with their melancholy whine, then moved on to caress that ethereal, all-seeing moon. While she kissed the man she was falling in love with all over again.

Chapter Fifteen

The moon followed them all the way back across the city and onto the bay bridge into Fleur. But it was a midnight moon now, high in the sky and still smiling down on them. In that light, they'd reached a gentle truce that seemed more forbidden and intimate than all the flirting in the years past.

Julien smiled over at her, a sureness and awareness in his eyes. He considered this a successful evening, she reckoned.

Well, so did she.

Alma hated to go into her tiny cottage alone, and that rankled her. She'd always loved her little house. This had been her grandmother Blanchard's house. Her daddy and her aunts and uncles had been raised here. After Grand-mère passed, everyone wanted to tear it down. But she begged her daddy to let her redo it and live here since it was so near the café. She'd never felt lonely here before.

Now she wanted Julien to come and sit with her on the couch by the tiny little fireplace, maybe read her a poem or tell her a funny fishing story. She wanted to cook him dinner and laugh with him while they cleaned the kitchen and put away the dishes.

She wanted so many things, things that she'd long ago given up on dreaming about. And that hurt as much as it thrilled her.

She was still afraid.

"You're frowning," Julien said as he walked her to the door. "Indigestion, or are you tired of me?"

She laughed up at him. "I'm not tired and no, I don't have indigestion. But I think I did eat too much."

He leaned close, his smile bittersweet. "But you're still trying to figure us out, right?"

Apparently he knew her better than she gave him credit for. "I think so. You know I never make rash decisions."

"*Oui,* I sure know that. I've been waiting almost ten years for you to make a move back toward me."

That statement floored her and touched her. "So all this time, you figured I'd wise up one day and want you back?"

"*Non,* I didn't figure. I hoped and prayed."

"You have remarkable resolve and restraint, Mr. LeBlanc."

"Not really. But I can be a patient man. If something's worth waiting for, that is."

"I hope I don't disappoint you."

"Is that a warning?"

She touched a hand to his face. "No. Just a concern. I'd never want to disappoint you again, Julien."

He tugged her into his arms. "You've never done that."

"I think I did that night long ago. I never realized that I had a big part in your actions that night."

He touched her hair, tugged at her wrap. "I told you it doesn't matter now. Let's forget the past and move toward the future. Our future."

She hugged him close and, for a moment, enjoyed the comfort of his strong arms. "I'll need some time. I want this to work, if God means for it to work."

"I'm praying He does. I'm praying you want me as much as I want you."

She lifted her head, her eyes touching on his. "I'm praying, too. But right now, I need to get inside and go to sleep. Morning comes early around here."

"*Oui.* I've kept you out long enough. And we do have that festival meeting tomorrow night."

"Oh, I'd forgotten," she replied, amazed that he seemed to be serious about his duties on the committee. "I guess I'll see you then."

"If not before," he said. Then he gave her a long good-night kiss that sent delightful little sparks all the way to her toes.

"Good night," she managed to squeak out. She had a hard time making her key fit the lock.

Julien stood back then grabbed the keys and opened the door for her. Before she could get inside, he tugged her back for a quick peck on her lips. "I had a good time."

"Me, too. Thank you. I'll see you tomorrow."

He watched until she'd shut the door.

Alma leaned into that door, taking a deep breath. Then she went to the window and saw him standing under the big cypress tree. She waved and he waved back. Then he turned and walked to his truck.

Alma wanted to sink down on the floor and stay there in a bundle all night.

"What have I done?" she asked herself. "What should I do now?"

So much had happened in a few short weeks. All these years she'd been spinning around like a little top, just out of Julien's reach. Alma always knew he was there, always felt she could turn to him if she ever needed him.

She'd always needed him.

He'd hugged her during her mother's illness and death, somehow managing to maintain a quiet, respectful distance each time he brought food or called to check. He'd asked about Callie all throughout Callie's illness and her divorce. Julien had helped rebuild the café after the last hurricane, vowing to make it strong and sturdy again. He'd supplied her with part of his catch of the day almost every day, giving her the best of his haul, sharing and taking her money to pay so neither of them would be insulted.

Julien had always been nearby, for her. She'd tried to be a friend to him, too.

But now, oh, now things were so different. She'd been walking around in a veil of muted distortion for years, wearing her blinders so she didn't have to look too closely at her own torment and loneliness.

But tonight her eyes were wide open. Tonight, she'd seen a new Julien, a more serious Julien who did have hopes and dreams and aspirations. Hopes that included her. Dreams that held her.

What would it be like, to be his wife, to have his children, to spend the rest of her time on earth with Julien?

That was the big question.

She knew in her heart she wanted that dream,

but she had to be realistic, too. Dreams were one thing. Reality was a whole other issue.

So she went to her room, got dressed for bed, curled up underneath the mosquito netting and prayed that she'd make the right decision.

Because if she turned him away this time, Julien would not be back.

And their delicate friendship would be over forever.

Julien waited at the door of the fellowship hall the next evening and watched for Alma to cross the street. She was late.

Maybe she wasn't coming. Maybe last night had been a big mistake.

But she'd kissed him. Several times.

Kissing him didn't mean she was in love with him, though, he reminded himself. Winning Alma back would be a long, drawn-out progress. He was in this for the long haul.

Somebody thumped him on the back of the head and he whirled, ready to knock right back. "Tebow, what's your problem?"

"You," Tebow said with a grin. "If you'd take your eyes off that little house across the street, you might notice other people coming and going around here."

"I see you," Julien replied. He rubbed his head. "Now I'll get a headache."

"You will not. If you do get any kind of ache, it'll be coming from your lovesick heart."

"When did you get back into town and why are you at this meeting?" Julien asked to change the subject.

"I got back last night," Tebow said as he nodded toward a few other committee members making their way toward the refreshment table inside. "And just in time to pass by Alma's house and see you two all cuddled up right there underneath the porch light."

"Is there a law against that?" Julien growled, his gaze shifting back to Alma's house. Sometimes living in a small town did have disadvantages.

Tebow kept grinning. "No. But such public displays of affection can only mean your charms are wearing down the pretty lady. Am I right?"

"I don't know," Julien said, shrugging. "We seem to be making progress, but Alma…she's a tough cookie."

"You can make that cookie crumble," Tebow said with such assurance Julien had to laugh.

"I don't know about that, bro."

"Here she comes," Tebow said, poking Julien so hard he almost fell off the short step into the building.

"Why are you here?" Julien asked again, hoping to look nonchalant when Alma walked up.

"My mama's got a head cold and she asked me to conduct the meeting and report back to her."

"Mercy on all of us, then," Julien replied. No telling what Tebow would forget to remember.

"Hey," Alma said as she approached them. "Are y'all the welcoming committee?"

"He is," Tebow said. "Me, I'm just here to read off the five pages of instructions my mama gave to me from her sick bed. She has a cold."

"Oh, I'll have to send her some soup," Alma said, giving Julien a quiet smile. "Ready to get started?"

"Sure." But he held back. "How are you today?"

"Good," she said on a low whisper. "I missed you at breakfast…and lunch."

"I had to go talk to a lawyer about Pierre," he explained, his mood turning grim. "Charged me money I don't have, but what else can I do?"

"What did the lawyer say?"

"He'll try to get probation and community service since it's a first offense. Pierre was over the legal limit, so he does need to learn his lesson."

"That might be good for Pierre. Serving others always makes a person appreciate their own circumstances."

"I'm not sure Pierre worries about others enough to appreciate anything," Julien admitted. "But he is toeing the line for now." He took some of her folders as they headed toward the meeting table. "We've had some good talks, though. I took Pretty Mollie's advice and tried to talk to him more and to listen more to what he says back."

"You love your brother."

It was a fact and she said it as such. "Yes, I do. But mostly I don't want to see my mother hurt."

Her smile showed her understanding…and their new friendship, relationship, whatever-ship. "You're a good man, Julien."

"Am I?"

"Of course." She leaned close. "I had a great time last night."

"So…no regrets?"

"None so far. But the week's young."

Her grin took his breath away. "Well, then, let's get through this meeting so we can walk underneath the moon again before it turns into a sliver."

She bobbed her head, still grinning, and hurried to her side of the table. Julien handed her files over then went to get coffee.

"I think you've won her over," Tebow said on a covert mumble. "I haven't seen Alma grinning so much since she won the bread pudding contest at the festival two years ago."

"Will you kindly back off?" Julien suggested. "I thought you had a girl in New Orleans, so quit worrying about mine."

"Ah, well, I did *have* a girl but she decided not

to have me around anymore. She wants to explore her options. Go figure."

"Isn't that female-speak for 'Get lost, loser'?"

Tebow held out a hand. "You did not just say that to me!"

"I'm stating facts," Julien said. "That's what you always say when you break up with someone. You call yourself a loser."

"I am a loser," Tebow replied, a grimace centered on his face. "But I wasn't feeling it anyway." Then he looked over to where Alma was talking to another woman. "I envy you and Alma. Y'all have been in love since high school."

"We have not."

"Yes, you have."

"Tebow, it's time to start the meeting," Reverend Guidry said, motioning to them. "I believe you have your mother's notes."

Tebow winked at Julien then strolled across the room. "Yes, sir. I hope everyone's had refreshments. This is a long list."

Julien looked at Alma. She was busy scribbling in her own weighty notebook. Women sure took their busy work seriously.

He watched her, loving the way her brow lifted as she concentrated and the way she held her pen in mid-air while she read over her notes. He loved the way she dressed in floral dresses and skirts and cute little pastel tops with embellishment on them. He checked her feet and got a kick out of the wedged white tennis shoes with sparkly azure-blue laces.

"Julien, want to join us over here?" Reverend Guidry said with a big smile.

Julien looked up to find everyone staring at him.

Tebow was right. He'd been in love with the same woman since high school. He only hoped that woman had always been in love with him, too.

"I'll be right there."

He hurried to the table and settled in to discuss the upcoming festival. But it was hard to concentrate on ordering supplies and coordinating when to start setting up tents and tables when all he wanted to do was grab Alma and take her away with him like a pirate capturing a fair maiden.

She smiled at him, listened to his suggestions and answered his questions, all the while with a sweet smile on her pretty face. She responded to everyone else, assuring them it would all turn out wonderful. She gave Tebow a thorough update to pass on to his mother.

Alma was the real deal, entrenched in this community, solid in her faith and a strong supporter of Fleur and its struggling economy. And she was definitely, without a doubt, the woman he intended to spend the rest of his life with.

But in spite of how well this new plan seemed to be going, he still had to wonder—would the fair maiden want to run away with the likes of him?

Or more to the point—stay right here in Fleur with the likes of him?

Chapter Sixteen

The Saturday of the festival started out sunny and beautiful, even if the weather report indicated approaching storms.

Just before noon, Alma stood at the end of Highway 1 through town. An array of brightly colored striped tents lined the closed street, making it look like a giant ribbon floating between the bayou and the big canal that eventually flowed out into the bay and the Gulf. The smell of spicy boiled crawfish and smoked turkey legs and barbecue mingled with the sweet scent of funnel cakes and cotton candy.

Cars filled every available parking space and open spaces along the road on either side. People were mingling under the biggest tent, ready to hear some good zydeco music and dance later at the *fais do-do*. The children's area held colorful games and a giant blown-up alligator where they could jump and frolic inside the gator's belly. Right now, between eating at the many food booths and shopping at the arts and crafts booths, everyone seemed to be having a good time.

She felt a hand on her arm and turned to find Julien smiling at her. He held a funnel cake covered with cinnamon and powdered sugar. "Are you hungry?"

"Too busy to eat," she said, wishing she could sit under the tent with him and enjoy the music.

"C'mon, now," he said, dragging her off to the side underneath a shady live oak. "I know you've been up since dawn and I had Pierre and Sweet Mollie make this funnel cake just for us. They added extra cinnamon and some nutmeg for you."

"Did they now?" Alma brought off a chunk of the swirled fried dough. "You know this is full of sugar and starch, don't you?"

"*Oui,* and flour and grease and more sugar and nutmeg and cinnamon. So, your point?"

She laughed at his confused look. "It is good. Okay, maybe a couple of bites before I get back into the fray."

"What's left to do?" he asked, allowing her to take another big chunk of their treat. "My people are in place. I've got about fifteen teenagers lined up until closing time, and Pierre and Mollie are watching them for me."

"Are you sure that's a good idea?" Alma asked,

glancing down the food alley with a tight smile. "Remember when we were young? You have to stay with them at all times, Julien."

His overexaggerated grimace almost made her laugh. "I'm hovering nearby and helping as needed. Pierre won't let them abandon their posts. We've got plenty of supplies and more inside the church pantry. I've got it under control, *catin*."

Alma didn't want him to think she couldn't trust him. She'd been working on that issue since their night in New Orleans. Since their newfound closeness. Since forever, it seemed. So instead of fretting and suggesting he get back to his post, she took another chunk of the curled dough and munched down on it.

"Aren't you supposed to test one of your boats out on the channel today?" she asked Julien. "I've seen people admiring them at the public dock all day."

"I am," he said while he dusted powdered sugar off his fingers. "Your daddy wants to take a ride in the skiff."

"My daddy?" Alma tried to swallow the dough that was suddenly lodged in her throat. "I thought you two were just teasing me about that. You can't actually be serious?"

"Completely serious. He said he wanted to test out the wooden skiff. Said he's had a hankering for a new one."

"He has a sailboat that holds almost twenty people. Why does he need a new skiff?"

"Maybe he wants one so he can be alone out on the water sometimes without having to take out that big boat full of tourists. That's his job. This can be his fun, on his own time. He has a trolling motor he can use."

"Maybe." Alma felt uneasy, the too-sweet food she'd just eaten hitting her stomach with a thud. "I can't wrap my brain around you and my papa out on a boat together. A very small boat, I might add."

"Are you afraid he'll try to drown me?"

"Maybe. He's still a tad perturbed about us."

"Have you told him anything more about us," Julien asked. Then he held up a hand. "I mean, whatever this is between us at least?"

"I haven't had a chance to sit down and explain," she hedged. "We usually have Sunday dinner together out at the house, but Callie was there last time I went out and he'd invited the neighbors over. I didn't think I should bring it up."

"So you're still not sure yourself?"

She saw the frustration and disappointment in his eyes. "He knows enough, Julien. Just enough to leave us alone and let us figure things out. We're adults, after all."

"Okay. I guess I can live with that."

She wished she hadn't been so apprehensive

about the boat ride before, but Alma didn't want her daddy to get overly excited. His health wasn't the best. "I'm sure it'll be okay," she finally told Julien. "You know how he gets, though. Don't let him provoke you."

"Your papa and I have an understanding," Julien replied. He threw their now empty paper plate into a nearby recycling can. "I understand that if I hurt you again, he will probably kill me. He understands that if I hurt you again, he will surely kill me."

She laughed at that. "You don't look too terrified."

He leaned close, the scent of cinnamon all around him. "That's because I'm not going to hurt you, ever. I'm rowing as fast as I can to prove that, darlin'."

Alma gave him a quick kiss. "You can slow down, then. You're doing okay in that area."

He kissed her on the nose. "And how about in this area?"

Delight danced down her spine. "Not bad there, either."

"Okay. I'm off to check on the vagabonds running my popcorn and cotton candy empire. Not to mention cooking my famous funnel cakes."

She laughed again at his smug tone. The man was adorable, no doubt about that. But would her daddy think the same?

Julien waved at her as he hurried to his assigned booths.

"Well, that was sure special," her sister said from behind her, her arms full of drink cups and extra napkins. "Now that you're done kissing and eating and flirting with Julien, want to help me get this stuff to the main food tent?"

Alma sighed. "Sure. I have to check on the gumbo anyway. Might be time to bring out another batch."

"It's selling at a brisk pace," Callie replied. "I think this is your best. How you got so much cooked in the past few days is beyond me."

Alma laughed. "Winnie helped and so did Mollie. And I haven't been sleeping much so I spent some extra time in the café, cooking it and then cooling it down."

"And you've got a whole slew of folks in there stirring away right now," Callie replied. "Think we'll go through twenty-five gallons today?"

"I've prepared for at least four hundred people, based on last year's estimations," Alma said while she waved and smiled to people she knew. "Seems we've got a bigger crowd this year."

"No storms, no spills, no floods," Callie retorted. "And a nice spring day."

"But rain later," Alma said with a thread of worry. "Maybe it'll hold off until tomorrow."

"Maybe," Callie said. "Hey, are you okay?"

Alma made a face. "Julien says Papa wants to take a ride out on the skiff he's got on display down by the docks. Why would our daddy want to go out for a boat ride today of all days? And with Julien?"

"They talked about this before, Alma. I think they're trying to get to know each other better, for your sake."

"Maybe so. I've just got this worried feeling in the pit of my stomach."

"That's not worry, honey," Callie replied. "You ate half a funnel cake. And that's probably the only meal you've had today, right?"

"You could be right," Alma admitted. "Maybe I need to find a sandwich or something."

"Good idea," Callie replied. "Okay, got that chore taken care of. I'm gonna check on my flower booth and see if any of my volunteers want a break. Then I might grab some of your gumbo and check out the jewelry booths. Wanna come along?"

Alma shook her head. "Do you really need another necklace?"

"No," Callie replied with a grin. "But I do need some new earrings."

Her sister loved jewelry as much as Alma loved bling on her tennis shoes. Brenna loved art, Callie loved jewelry and Alma loved cooking, along with shoes. Good thing they were all gainfully employed.

After she helped Callie with her supplies, Alma started back up the long alley of booths. When she passed the funnel cake booth, she saw Julien busy helping the four teenagers inside. But she didn't see Pierre and Mollie in any of the booths.

"Hey, Sara," she called to a cute blonde. "Where's your adult supervisor?"

"You mean Pierre?" the petite girl asked, grinning.

"That'd be the one," Alma replied, glancing toward Julien in the bigger booth. He was busy with a line of customers. "Where is Pierre?" she asked the girl again.

Sara, busy getting cotton candy for a little boy, said, "Oh, he and Mollie took a break. I think they went to get something to drink."

Alma didn't like that since they'd supplied each booth with plenty of water and soda so the volunteers wouldn't have to leave until their official breaks.

"Was it their scheduled break?" Alma asked.

Sara shrugged. "I don't know. Ask Emily."

Emily hurried across the booth with a corn dog. "I swapped with Pierre and he got Patrick to swap with Mollie. I think they were going to where Pierre's motorcycle is parked."

Alma shook her head. Pierre was neglecting his supervisor duties to show off his toy to Mollie. She wouldn't bother Julien with this. She'd go find them and ask them to return to their booths.

Taking off through the crowd of slow-moving people, Alma walked past the church parking lot and scanned the trees and bushes. Then she saw Pierre and Mollie sitting against his bike and Pierre had a beer in his hand.

Was Mollie drinking, too? It didn't look like it.

Alma walked up, trying to look nonchalant. "Hey, how y'all doing?"

Mollie straightened her spine, clearly embarrassed. "Oh, hi, Alma. What's up?"

"Nothing much. I just saw the kids in the corn dog and cotton candy booth. I was concerned they didn't have an adult supervisor."

Did she really sound like an old fuddy-duddy?

Apparently so, by the way Pierre looked at her.

"We took a break," he said. Then he took a sip of beer.

Alma didn't think it was her place to reprimand him, but she couldn't have him drinking around the underage teens either. "Pierre, you did know this is a nonalcoholic event, right?"

"That's why I brought my own," he said on a glib note.

Mollie shook her head. "I'm not drinking, Alma. I just took a five-minute break to see Pierre's bike."

Alma wasn't sure how to handle this. She normally didn't get into other people's business, but this festival was geared toward families. Any heavy drinking was done off the premises, away from the church and the busy booths. The police rarely had to arrest anyone for public drinking. She didn't want Pierre to get into even more trouble. He was on probation, which surely meant he shouldn't be drinking at all.

"Pierre," she said, hoping to convince him, "you don't want to get arrested again. Could you put the beer away for now and get back to your booth?"

He appeared sullen, but he nodded. Then he drained the rest of the beer and tossed the bottle into a nearby trash can. "Julien made me do this. I really don't like frying corn dogs."

Mollie looked shocked. "The money goes toward upkeep for the town park and to help people who lost their homes in the last hurricane. It's for a good cause."

Pierre didn't change his mood. "Maybe I don't care about good causes."

The hurt look on Mollie's face said it all. "I can't believe you just said that."

Pierre's expression changed from grouchy to perplexed. And a little unsure. But he used a bit of surly to cover it. "I don't know why. With me, what you see is what you get. All this do-good stuff didn't save my daddy."

Alma pulled Mollie by the arm. "C'mon. I think he's had too much to drink and he'll regret talking to you that way when he's sober."

Mollie halted though. "No, he's just hurting. I shouldn't leave him."

Pierre glared at them. "No, go ahead. I'm a loser. I'm a drunk. I don't know why I thought you'd be different."

"I didn't say that," Mollie said, her tone rising.

Alma looked around to see a group of people watching them.

She had to do something before Julien saw this. He'd only make matters worse by getting into an argument with his brother.

"Pierre, let's go inside the church. It's getting a little hot out here."

"I don't want to go in the church," he said, his hands out in protest. "I want to take my girl for a ride on my bike."

"I can't go," Mollie said. "Not with you drinking."

At least the girl had a good head on her shoulders.

Alma tried again. "Pierre, you're not a loser but you've been drinking. Let's just go inside—"

"I said no," he shouted. "Now get out of my face."

The next thing Alma knew she was being pushed aside in a rush of air and breath. A figure whirled by so fast, she had to grab hold of Mollie to keep from falling.

Julien had his little brother by the collar, dragging him toward the back door of the church. "You will not disrespect these two women, do you hear me?"

He shot Alma and Mollie an apologetic look, then opened the door to the educational wing and pushed his brother inside.

Alma looked at Mollie. The girl burst into tears.

And right at that moment, the sky went dark as a big rain cloud covered the sun.

Chapter Seventeen

Julien couldn't believe his brother was drinking on a Saturday morning. And inside the church parking lot at that.

"What were you thinking?" he asked Pierre, his tone as crusty and dry as the shells scattered across the church driveway. "It's bad enough you drink at night and on weekends, but here, now! I asked you to help me. I thought you'd learned something from getting arrested, Pierre."

"You didn't ask me to work," Pierre snarled. "You demanded that I get up and help you. That's what you always do—boss me around like I'm a kid. I didn't come here because of you, though. I only came because Mollie wanted me to."

Wondering what had happened to their new understanding, Julien grunted. "Well, good luck with explaining to Mollie why you're acting like an oaf, too."

Pierre hung his head and glared at Julien. "I don't care. I don't want to be here. This crowd is a drag."

Julien didn't know how to convince him. "This crowd includes your neighbors and friends and the people who make this town what it is. This crowd is full of tourists who fish these waters and eat at our restaurants and help our economy. Can't you see that?"

"I don't care about that," Pierre shot back. "Our daddy worked hard to please the tourists and this town and now he's dead. Dead, Julien, at fifty-seven. Or have you forgotten his birthday?"

Julien's anger evaporated like a mist of humidity on a strong wind. "I haven't forgotten, bro. And I miss him as much as you do. But we need to honor his memory by doing the best we can. I need you to remember what Papa taught us. He showed us how to work hard and enjoy life. He wanted us to do right by people and live our lives with dignity and integrity and a strong faith. That's what we have to do, Pierre. We have to honor him."

Pierre slumped against a wall, his eyes red-rimmed and bleary. "It doesn't matter. I tried not to drink but things are just boring around here. I guess Mollie's done with me now."

Julien's heart ached for his brother. He'd been in this same spot the night Alma told him she never wanted to see him again. Told him to clean up his act and grow up.

He'd surely done that. He'd aged a lifetime after his father's death. And he was adding the years by the minute, standing here watching his little brother mess up his life.

"You can change," he told Pierre now. "You can start over again. We can get you some help. You don't have to drink to get rid of the pain, Pierre."

"Yes, I do." Pierre lifted himself off the wall then dropped his big hands to his side. "I start out feeling good, but—"

"But when you wake up, you don't feel so hot, right?"

"Right. I want to wipe it all away. That's why I drink. And then, I feel lousy so I drink some more."

"You can stop that. I know you can."

"No, I can't," Pierre said. "I can't. It's too late. I don't know anything else, bro. I don't know how to stop. I can't feel anything when I drink. I don't want to feel like I felt when they buried our daddy. And I'm tired of you telling me what to do. You're not my daddy."

He gave Julien one last look then took off, slamming the door back against the building so hard it rattled. Julien ran out after him. "Pierre, don't get on that bike."

His brother waved his hand in the air and kept on going back into the sea of people walking around.

Julien watched Pierre disappear into the crowd. Letting out a hard sigh, he searched for Alma and Mollie. He saw them sitting on a bench away from the crowd.

Alma got up as he approached. "How is he?"

"Not good. He took off. At least he didn't get on his bike."

Mollie looked up at him, her expression full of worry and fear. "I can't date your brother if he keeps getting drunk, Julien. He told me he had stopped. I like him a lot, but I'm not ready for this. It's like dating two different people. Sometimes he's so sweet and considerate, but when he's drinking, he gets all belligerent and mean."

"You don't have to handle this," Julien said. "It's not your problem, Mollie. I'll take care of my brother." He looked at Alma, his heart pumping angst and misery. "And maybe one day he'll wake up and realize he's making a big mistake. He'll see that his actions have cost him a lot more than a night in jail."

Alma held his gaze, her eyes wide with worry and wonder. "Julien, what can I do to help?"

"Pray," he said. "And get someone else to handle my booths. I've got to find Pierre and take him home."

Alma found some adults to fill in for Julien the rest of the afternoon. She was working a two-hour shift herself when a distinguished-looking, big-boned man with thick gray hair approached her.

"How can I help you?" she asked in a cheerful tone, taking in the man's white button-up shirt and khaki trousers. She didn't want her worries about Julien and Pierre to show, but she hadn't seen either of them since Pierre had taken off.

"Are you Alma Blanchard?" the man asked with a smile, his dark brown eyes bright.

"Yes. That's me." She glanced around the booth then asked one of the teens to man the window for a while. "I'll be right out." Maybe he knew something about Pierre.

She came around the counter and smiled at the man. "What can I do for you?"

The man extended his hand. "I'm Jacob Sonnier. I'm from Georgia and I write a syndicated food column called 'Ain't That Good?' Goes out to several papers across the South. I've also written several Southern cookbooks."

Alma bobbed her head. She'd heard of him all right. He'd been a chef in an upscale restaurant in Atlanta before opening his own restaurant in Baton Rouge, and now he was famous for being on talk shows and cooking shows. "I read your column all the time and I've tried a lot of your recipes. My sister Brenna gave me one of your cookbooks for Christmas. It's so nice to meet you."

"Same here, little lady. And Brenna's the one who sent me. She comes into my restaurant in Baton Rouge all the time. But she kept on bragging about you, so I had to find you. Had me the best bowl of gumbo earlier and they told me you cooked it."

Beaming, Alma grinned. "I did, but I had a lot of help. It's my mother's recipe, passed down from her mother. We've been making that gumbo in the Fleur Café for three generations now."

"It's mighty good, mighty good," Jacob said, his jowls jiggling with each *mighty*. "Have you ever considered selling it in a mass-market capacity?"

Alma didn't know what to say. "No, not really. I don't have the proper equipment for something that big. It takes all I can do to cook this batch for the festival every year."

"Well, that's why I wanted to talk to you. I know all kinds of food distributors who can help you process it and sell it. I'm thinking you could go regional and then national."

Alma had to process his suggestion. "I'm not sure I want to change the recipe. Preservatives might do that."

"No, you wouldn't have to change anything. We'd freeze it and ship it right out."

Her heart beat a happy tune. This was part of her dream. If she mass produced her gumbo recipe, she might be able to pick and choose a place to work. But why would she want to do that now? she thought, an image of Julien in her mind.

"I'm not sure," she told Jacob Sonnier. "I'd have to find out the details regarding everything about this. It's a big step."

"Of course." Mr. Sonnier handed her his card. "Just let me do some figuring and make some calls. That's my number. I'll get back to you. I'm sure gonna write about this festival in my next column. And I'd like to interview you at length, too. You and me might be able to write a cookbook together." He took out another card. "Write down your number if you don't mind."

Alma jotted her cell number on the card then put his extra card in her apron pocket. "Thanks. I appreciate it." She smiled up at him. "I've often thought I'd like to open my own restaurant in New Orleans or maybe even another big city, but I stay so busy here I haven't had a chance to go back to school and learn the business end of things. I'm not a fancy chef, but I do love to cook."

Mr. Sonnier's belly laugh caused several nearby people to stare. "Suga', you got the best thing going right here. Why would you want to give up that quaint little café for some big-city chain restaurant? Trust me, it looks glamorous, but it's a lot of hard work."

"Good point," she said, shaking his hand. Hadn't she just thought the same thing herself? She stared down at his card, all sorts of possibilities sprouting like water lilies in her head. "But mass producing my gumbo sure would bring in some much-needed revenue. I could at least update the café and add another dining room." Then another idea struck her. "I could open the distribution center right here in Fleur. That would give people jobs."

"Good thinking, but let's not get ahead of ourselves. Lots to think about and plan, but hometown jobs are always a plus. I'll be in touch." He shook her hand again. "So nice to meet you, Alma. I'm gonna take me a big cup of that gumbo for the road. I'll tell your sister I talked to you, too."

"Thanks again," Alma said. She'd have to call Brenna and ask her about this. Her sister liked to play "boss" sometimes. Was this Brenna's way of giving Alma a chance at that life she'd always dreamed about, or was Brenna trying to sabotage Alma's getting back with Julien? "I appreciate this so much."

"I'll call you soon," Mr. Sonnier replied. Then

he strolled off through the crowd, waving and chatting with people.

"Friendly fellow," Alma mumbled as she headed back into the booth, her feet not quite meeting the earth. The lunch rush was over now. The afternoon crowd flowed at a steady pace, giving the booth workers a little breathing time. But where was Julien? She couldn't wait to tell him about this.

He couldn't find Pierre.

Julien searched the docks and the marina, then backtracked down the row of booths, checking the ones where Pierre was supposed to be working. Mollie was in the cotton candy booth, her expression solemn. When he didn't see Pierre there, he kept moving. But he did notice Alma talking to a tall, stocky man. He looked in the park and near the bayou. Pierre's bike was still in the same spot, parked and locked. He asked around but no one had seen his brother. Their mama would be here soon. She'd planned to come to the *fais do-do* to listen to the music. But she'd be expecting both of her sons to be in attendance, too.

"Where are you, Pierre?"

Julien felt a tap on his back and whirled, hoping to see his brother. Alma smiled at him.

"Any luck?"

"No," he said. "I've looked everywhere, even

called the Backwater. He's not there. If he left, he left on foot. His bike is still here."

She brushed her hand over his arm, the touch as gentle as a wisp of silk against his skin. "Maybe he just needed to find a quiet spot to cool off."

"Maybe." Julien had hoped this would be a good day. He'd actually enjoyed working with the kids in the food booths. Reverend Guidry had been great to work with and get to know more. And the hand-built boats he had on display at the marina were getting a heavy buzz. "I'm sorry I haven't done my job, Alma."

Her face twisted in surprise. "What are you talking about? The youth group kids are working hard and they've all been prompt and willing to switch out shifts. So far, so good."

"But I'm not there to supervise, the way you told me."

"It's okay. I found some help. You have to take care of Pierre."

He let out a weary sigh, frustration hitting at him like lapping waves. "I'm so tired of this. He told me I'm not his daddy."

"Well, you're not, but you are his older brother." She reached up to brush away his bangs, her touch like a balm of soothing relief. "You can't nag him or preach to him, Julien. We both remember how that feels."

He caught her hand in his. "*Oui,* but what else can I do? I've tried listening. I've tried understanding. I've tried talking. And I've prayed."

"Give him some time. It's hard when we lose a loved one. He's hurting the same as you. Maybe more. He's acting out."

"You can say that again." Julien took her hands in his, the need to wrap his arms around her and hold her forever pushing through him. "How are you?"

"I'm okay," she said. Then she pulled a card out of her apron. "I got a possible offer to mass produce my gumbo. You know, to sell in grocery stores." She handed Julien the card. "And—"

He looked down at the card. "A chef?" He read the card, his tired, bruised heart cracking another inch or two. "Jacob Sonnier, Southern chef, cookbook author, columnist and owner of Sonnier's Southern Food in New Orleans and Baton Rouge." The name and bio were followed by the column heading: "Ain't That Good?"

Julien stopped, the one thought that had held him back for ten years shouting in his head. She'd said something about her gumbo, but all he could hear or see was that she still wanted to leave Fleur. And him. "You talked to a chef?" he asked again, his voice low.

Smiling, she backed away. "Yes, but—"

Julien schooled his reaction, while his heart

seemed to crack like broken shells. "And what did this chef have to offer you, sweetheart? Something good, I hope."

She pushed at her hair, her eyes a misty blue. "He…uh…is interested in possibly mass-producing my gumbo to sell in local stores."

Julien ignored the little tremors of fear and regret inside his soul. He couldn't shout out to her not to do this. He couldn't tell her this might be her escape route right up Highway 1. He couldn't hold her back.

So he smiled, pulled her close and held her there, his eyes closed to what might happen next. "That's wonderful. That's good. This is your big chance. And we both know you deserve this. I hope it works out for you."

Alma stared down at the business card then looked back up at Julien, wondering about his reaction. He'd tempered things for her sake, but she could see the doubt and the regret in his dark eyes. He wouldn't hold her back. She knew that. He'd let her go because he thought she deserved this more than he deserved her.

"It's a great opportunity," she said, hoping to reassure him. "And I'd be able to stay here in Fleur and oversee things. I could use the money. This town could use the money."

"*Oui,* you do have to consider that. It's great. It's just that the timing is kind of lousy."

He was one to talk about bad timing. "When is a good time, then, Julien? I've been right here, waiting for ten long years. I could have left but I didn't."

She saw the flash of anger in his eyes. "No, you didn't. But you didn't hang around for *me,* Alma. You stayed out of a sense of duty to your family. Did you ever think about me at all?"

"You know I did," she said, her hand on his arm. "And now, Julien, we have a chance to make things right. We can do this."

"Not if you settle for *me,*" he said, stepping back.

How could she tell him she wanted him, only him? Nothing else was that important. How could she make him see his worth?

"Julien…"

"We'll talk more later." He kissed her and touched a hand to her hair. "I have to get back to looking for my brother."

They were right back where they'd started so many years ago, Alma thought after Julien stomped away. She was so concerned about him and his brother and how he'd handle things if she took this opportunity, she didn't notice the gathering clouds or the raindrops on her face.

She wished they'd had time to really discuss

this, but Julien was already backing away, jumping to the wrong conclusions. But if he had listened, if he'd given her a moment to breathe, she would have told him this was the best thing for both of them.

Because as she'd tried to explain, this would mean she'd be able to provide more for her family but also provide for her workers and this town, too. This would be the realization of one of her dreams, a solution, a blessing that could change her life.

And it *would* mean she could stay here with Julien.

Alma hurried down the tent alley, the rain hitting her and people rushing by her to find shelter, and accepted that Julien had won. He'd forced her to fall in love with him again.

But would he turn away and break her heart all over again, too?

Chapter Eighteen

Julien wanted to take back his less-than-lackluster reaction. He shouldn't have gotten all hot and bothered by what Alma had told him. She had a talent for cooking and someone had finally noticed that. He should be happy for her. Instead, aggravated and worried over his little brother, he'd practically snapped at her to go ahead and take this as a sign to leave, finally leave, and he knew that had hurt her. Because he was so afraid he might lose her, it was like déjà vu all over again.

You never had her, he reminded himself as the rain hit at him like slivers of glass. The wind picked up, causing several of the lightweight plastic chairs underneath the big tent to dance across the concrete. Anything that wasn't held down became airborne in the heavy, straight-line wind. He watched as plastic bags, cups and small tree limbs flew by. People were huddled together, trying to keep dry. Cars and trucks filled with occupants as everyone waited out the storm.

But the rain kept falling.

Julien kept searching for Pierre, even when his heart was with Alma. He should go and apologize to her. Hurrying toward the cluster of booths, he glanced around. The kids were all gone, probably inside the church. Lightning flashed in a nasty zigzag across the sky. He looked for Alma, but she was nowhere in sight.

Should he go inside the church to find her? Maybe she'd gone back to the café. He needed to find Alma. He needed to find his brother. His mama expected him to take care of Pierre. She depended on him, looked to him as the head of their ragtag household.

Julien turned toward the docks and the marina. At least he could make sure his boats were safe, and maybe he'd find Pierre down there horsing around with his friends. But when he got down to the marina, his heart stopped cold.

The skiff was missing.

Alma watched from the café as sheets of hard rain marched across the main thoroughfare in perfect precision. The wind pushed at the rain, forcing it to drain into the nearby gutters and bayous. The whole town was a soaked mess, dark clouds crowding around where, minutes ago, people had been crowded. It looked like there wouldn't be a street dance tonight.

"We're running out of coffee," Winnie said from the kitchen. "Want me to make another pot?"

Alma nodded, her mind on Julien. Was he out there somewhere searching for his brother? Pushing away the dark thoughts and the pain of his grudging resolve earlier, she went back to work. The café was crowded with people who'd managed to get out of the rain before the storm had set in. She'd fed most of them, kept their glasses and cups full of tea and coffee, and now she just wanted to go home, have a cup of tea and call it a day.

Mollie glanced at the front door then looked over at Alma. The girl was sullen and sad, obviously worried about Pierre. But Mollie was made of strong stuff. She went about her job and stayed to herself.

Callie came in the back door, her umbrella dripping. "Have you seen Papa, Alma?"

Alma turned, her still-wet sneakers squeaking. "Not since this morning when he helped me move chairs. I thought he was going down to the marina to hang out with the other fishermen."

Callie's frown created a mark between her wide eyes. "No one's seen him for a while now. Most of them are inside out of the rain now, but Papa isn't at any of his usual hangouts."

"Have you called him?" Alma grabbed her phone out of her pocket. "No messages."

Callie came to stand close. "He's not answering his phone. I'm getting a little worried."

Alma glanced out into the rain. "You'd think he'd come here to wait out the storm."

She hit her father's number and waited for him to answer. Then she shook her head. "That's strange. It didn't even go to voice mail. It didn't really do anything. I didn't hear a ring."

Callie pushed at her wet hair. "Something isn't right."

Alma didn't want to panic, but she was already worried about Julien. Now her father, too.

Then she went cold, her heart thumping. She grabbed Callie's arm. "They were going out in the skiff. Papa and Julien."

Callie cast a worried gaze out the window. "They wouldn't go out in this."

"But Julien might have gone out before the storm. We had a discussion and he walked away. I don't know where he went. What if he took Papa out?"

Callie shook her head. "Julien would know better."

Alma had to agree with that. Then her stomach went as cold as the rest of her. "But Pierre…

he's been missing all afternoon. Callie, what if *he* took Papa out on the skiff?"

Mollie's head came up and she dropped the handful of utensils she'd been putting away. "I haven't seen Pierre since we had our fight this morning."

Both sisters grabbed raincoats and headed for the door. Alma shouted to Winnie, "We've got to find Papa. Hold down the fort."

"I'll be here," Winnie said, worry heavy in her words. "We'll all be praying."

He needed to pray like he'd never prayed before.

Julien stood underneath an awning at the marina, his whole body shaking with a worrisome fear that only reminded him of the day his daddy had gone missing.

Tebow ran up to him. "Got your message. You think Pierre took the skiff?"

"I don't know, but he's been missing for hours. Somebody had to see him leave."

Tebow squinted toward the black heavens. "Bad time to be out on that water, bro."

"I know." Julien tried Pierre's phone again. No answer. "We have to go look for him. Can you help me round up some boats?"

"I'm on it," Tebow said, his phone near his ear.

"I'll call my cousin Pee-Bob. He's good at tracking people."

Julien didn't want to know how Pee-Bob tracked people in the rain. He just wanted to find his brother safe.

Tebow went around talking to several people who'd just arrived back at the marina.

Finally, he came back to shake his head at Julien.

"He took the skiff, Jule. And Alma's daddy was with him." Tebow's solemn scowl told the tale. "The old-timers said your brother was upset. Mr. Blanchard tried to calm him down. Pierre went out onto the dock and hopped in the skiff. Mr. Blanchard got in, too. Wouldn't bulge. They took off just before the storm hit."

Julien's stomach roiled and kicked. This was not good, not good at all. His brother had taken the skiff out into the storm. And Ramon Blanchard had been in the boat with him. Why would Mr. Blanchard get in a boat when he knew a storm was coming? Something wasn't right here.

He had to go and find them. Lifting the collar on the poncho he'd grabbed from inside the marina office, he headed toward the marina manager's boat. They'd have to alert the Coast Guard, too.

"Julien?"

He heard someone calling his name then turned to see Alma running toward him, Callie behind her. She took one look at his face and crumbled against her sister. "No. Julien, no."

Julien rushed to her, grabbed her close. "Look, they're both experienced boaters, *chère*. We don't know anything yet. They're probably high and dry. I'm going to find them. You know I'll find them."

Her eyes burned an angry, worried blue. "But Pierre was drinking. He could be even drunker than he was this morning."

"I understand that," Julien said, his prayers stuck in a revolving cycle. "We have to pray he wasn't. We have to pray they pulled up under a tree or made it to solid ground before the storm hit."

"Papa wanted to take that new boat out into the big water," Callie shouted over the thunder and wind. "What if he asked Pierre to do that?"

Julien had already wondered about that based on what some of the marina workers had heard. "I don't know. We have people who saw both of them get in the boat. I need to get out and look for them."

"I'm going with you," Alma said, rushing past him.

"No, *chère, non*." He wouldn't take that risk. "You can't do that. You need to go back to the café. I'm gonna call some of the other fisherman and boaters. They know these waters. We'll alert the Coast Guard, too. We'll find them."

She shook her head. "Julien, you'd tell me, wouldn't you? You'd tell me if anything bad had happened?"

"I'd tell you, *oui*." He motioned to Callie. "Take her back to the café and wait there. I'll call as soon as I hear anything."

Callie bobbed her head. "Any distress signals?"

"Nothing yet."

They stared each other down. Julien knew what Alma's sister was thinking, but he couldn't voice it. He couldn't even think it.

"I'll find them," he said to Alma. "I promise."

She twisted from her sister and ran to him. "Please, Julien. Please." Then she gave him a look that tore at him with the same intensity as the rain hitting them.

He kissed her and turned to hurry to the boat Tebow and the marina boss had readied for him. When he turned back, Alma was standing in the rain watching him, her tears mingling with the storm's fury.

The sight broke Julien in half.

He headed out into the dark waters and prayed he'd find his brother and her father alive and well. Because if he didn't, they'd never recover from this. No one would recover from this.

* * *

Alma stared at the iris on the counter. It was blooming. She'd need either to plant it or store it until the fall. She wanted to plant it. She wanted it to bloom and spread and grow in her garden. She wanted summer and sunshine and laughter.

She wanted her papa.

She wanted Pierre to be okay.

She wanted Julien.

She couldn't take her eyes away from that iris.

"C'mon, honey. Sit down."

Alma shook her head, ignored Winnie's hand on her arm.

"I'm okay. I'm okay." She glanced at the clock. "It's almost midnight. It's been hours. Where are they, Winnie?"

"I don't know, *chère,*" Winnie said on a whisper. "The Coast Guard is out there. Our men are out there. They'll find them. We have to believe that."

Outside, thunder boomed an ugly, loud answer. Lightning crashed and sizzled. The wind moaned its displeasure and its despair.

Callie walked up, her hair tugged into a lopsided coil on top of her head. "Alma, Julien's mama is here. Her sister brought her. She…she wanted to see you."

Alma's throat filled with a lump of regret and longing. She whirled to see Virginia LeBlanc slowly making her way toward the long counter. "Mrs. LeBlanc…"

Virginia tugged Alma into her arms and whispered words to her, sweet words as old as time in the Cajun French they both knew so well. "We need to pray together, belle. My *bébés* are out there, my *bébés*. Your papa, he's a strong, good man. Your Julien, he loves you so much. Did he tell you that?"

Alma had been so strong, so quiet up until that moment. But the tears began to flow and then she couldn't stop them. She cried and cried, there on Virginia LeBlanc's strong, motherly shoulder. She didn't realize how long she'd held these feelings deep inside. Her tears raged like the rain that kept coming outside, her heart crashed and danced like the lightning that crackled through the trees. The grief over losing her mother mingled with the hurt and confusion of losing Julien. What if he didn't come back to her? What if she never saw her sweet papa again? What if Mrs. Laborde lost colorful, crazy Tebow? What if Virginia lost both her sons? How could she live with that?

"I love him, too," she finally said. "I love Julien but I didn't tell him that. We had a misunderstanding. I should have told him."

"It's okay, *chère,*" Mrs. LeBlanc said on a soothing coo. "It's all okay. He knows you love him. He knows."

When she finally looked up, the restaurant was empty except for Callie, Winnie, Mollie, Mrs. LeBlanc's sister and Reverend Guidry.

"Let me take y'all to Alma's house, honey," Callie finally said. "We'll wait there, okay?"

Alma nodded, drained and exhausted. She might be able to make it through this long, dark night if she had her sister nearby. And Virginia LeBlanc. Mrs. LeBlanc was so strong, so forgiving. Why hadn't Alma been the same?

Mollie walked up to Alma, her apron in her hand. "Can I come and sit with y'all, just for a little while?"

"Of course, honey." She stood on wobbly legs and nodded. Then she turned and grabbed her iris. "I'm ready."

"Okay," Callie said, her own eyes red-rimmed and swollen. "Okay."

The little group locked up the restaurant and moved to Alma's house. Callie and Winnie pulled out blankets and towels to make everyone cozy. Mollie made a pot of tea. The rain kept coming, its intensity sometimes making it hard to speak. The water pounded on the tin roof and sloshed off the awnings and gutters. Great dark puddles covered the yard and the streets. The bayou crept closer and closer to the floating dock and the shallow shores.

Each time a clap of thunder hit, Alma got a

horrible image of an empty skiff tossing in the deep waters just off the sound.

Where were they? Where was Julien?

Alma closed her eyes and repeated her prayers over and over again, asking for a safe return of those she loved.

"Why don't they call?" Virginia asked. She rocked back and forth, back and forth on the sofa.

Reverend Guidry cleared his throat. "I'm sure we'll hear something soon." He lowered his head in prayer.

Alma tried to follow his baritone voice while he asked God to spare these men, to bring them home to the women who loved them. She closed her eyes, wishing with all her heart she'd told Julien just once that she had always loved him, always.

Then she looked up at Callie. Her sister was crying, too. She rushed to sit down beside Alma. "I can't lose Papa. I can't. We've already lost our mother, Alma. I can't lose Papa, too."

Alma's heart hurt for her sister. Callie was so sweet and strong, and she'd been through more than most women who'd lived a lifetime longer than she had. And Brenna. They'd called her hours ago to let her know the news. Hopefully, she was with her friends and her fiancé in Baton Rouge.

"I need to call Brenna again," Callie said,

wiping her eyes. "She's probably wondering what we've heard since I called her earlier."

Before she could pull out her phone, the front door opened and Brenna rushed in. "Callie!"

Callie and Alma fell into their baby sister's arms. "We told you not to drive in this weather," Alma mumbled.

"I don't care," Brenna said. "I had to come. I couldn't stand not knowing. Any word?"

"No," Callie said, wiping her eyes. "Where's Jeffrey?"

Brenna shook her head. "He didn't want to come. And I don't want to talk about it."

Callie pushed at Brenna's wet auburn hair. "You drove here by yourself? That's more than an hour and a half trip."

"Almost three hours in this weather," Brenna said. "The roads are bad. Flooded, washed out, trees down. I wasn't sure I'd ever get here."

"It's so late," Alma said, glancing at the clock. "I'm glad you're okay."

Brenna kissed her sister. "What can I do?"

Alma glanced at Virginia. "Help me make up the guest room for Mrs. LeBlanc. She looks exhausted."

"Okay," Brenna said. She tossed her designer handbag on the kitchen counter and tugged her overnight case into a corner out of the way. "I'll get the linens."

Alma went to Virginia. "We're making up a bed so you can rest. I know you won't sleep, but you can at least lie down."

Virginia smiled and patted her hand. "Do you mind if my sister stays with me?"

"Of course not," Alma replied. "I don't want my sisters to leave, so I'm sure not gonna send Miss Martha away. She'll be good company for you. For all of us." She glanced at Mollie. "You're welcome to stay, too."

Mollie bobbed her head.

"Until we hear," Virginia said, tears in her eyes.

"Yes, until we hear."

Alma guided her to the bedroom down the hallway, her prayers mirroring the hope she saw in Julien's mother's eyes.

Until we have them back safe, Lord.

Chapter Nineteen

Alma came awake, disoriented and wondering why she was asleep in the wing chair. Then she remembered. Glancing around, she saw Brenna and Callie curled up on the sofa, their heads on opposite pillows, their feet almost touching as their toes peeked out from the chenille blanket they'd both tried to use for cover. Mollie lay sprawled on a folded blanket near the empty fireplace, another blanket tangled against her jeans.

Julien.

Papa.

Pierre.

Tebow and the others. Where were they?

Alma glanced at the clock. Five in the morning. And still no word. She checked her cell phone. Nothing.

Slowly, she moved to get up, every muscle in her body sore and screaming. Careful and sluggish, she made her way to the kitchen then looked out the back window. The rain had stopped, but the waters of the bayou had risen into her yard. Thankfully, this house was up on a hill and it had been built on sturdy six-foot-tall pillars on the back side. She didn't have to worry about flooding right now.

But she did have to worry about the loved ones still lost out there somewhere.

Please, Lord, let them be safe. Let them be safe.

She silently prayed this single prayer over and over as she went about making coffee and pulling frozen homemade cinnamon rolls out of the freezer. Then she tiptoed down the tiny hallway and checked on Mrs. LaBlanc and her sister Martha. They were asleep, thankfully.

Please, Lord, let them be safe.

"Alma?"

She whirled, startled by Brenna's soft call. "I'm here, honey."

Brenna crept into the kitchen. "Are you all right?"

"I'm fine. I want to hear something, anything. I can't take the waiting."

Brenna grabbed the cups Alma offered. "I won't leave until I know something. I want to see Papa with my own eyes."

Touched, Alma stopped to stare at her baby sister. Brenna had the best of all of them in her.

She had hints of Callie and their mother in the golden streaks coloring her honeyed auburn hair. But she had Alma's blue eyes and petite size. She also carried their father's stubborn gene. Maybe they all did.

"What's going on with you and Jeffrey?" Alma asked to take her mind off her worries.

"I think we're done," Brenna said after pouring two cups of the rich, dark coffee. She sipped her coffee, her head down.

Alma stopped buttering rolls. "Seriously?"

"He got mad when I wanted him to drive me here," Brenna said in a loud whisper. "My daddy is out there somewhere, hurt or worse, and the man I love doesn't think I need to be here. He didn't want our dinner with his important clients interrupted. He suggested I wait to hear." She put her cup down. "I left the restaurant and went home to grab an overnight bag. I didn't tell him where I was going and I didn't answer his text."

Alma took Brenna in her arms. "Honey, I'm so sorry. Sorry that you had to drive here alone in that storm and sorry that Jeffrey is so selfish and petty."

"How could I have loved him in the first place?" Brenna said on a sniff. "I thought he was perfect. You know, urbane and smart, so up-and-coming. But he's so stuck on himself he can't see me at all. He can't see beyond his own perfect nose. Which makes me so stupid."

Alma patted her sister's curly hair. "We've all done stupid."

She thought about Julien and wished for the thousandth time that she'd had more time with him yesterday. Wished he hadn't jumped to the wrong conclusion about everything. Wished he hadn't just walked away, all stoic and unyielding.

Yesterday. It seemed so long ago now. He'd promised her a dance at the *fais do-do*. They'd laughed, eaten funnel cake, kissed.

If only she could have one more dance with him, one more kiss, one more touch.

Brenna pulled back to stare at her. "They'll come home, Alma. They have to. Papa's capable of surviving anything. We all are."

Alma bobbed her head and wiped her eyes. "And Julien—he knows these waters. He knows what to do in an emergency."

"Yes, he does," Brenna said, her hand touching Alma's face, tracing her tears. "Alma, he loves you so much he'll do anything to get back to you. And when he does, hold tight. Hold tight. I only wish Jeffrey had loved me half that much."

The sisters hugged again.

Then Alma felt another arm on hers and saw Callie standing there. Their older sister wrapped her arms around each of them for a group hug. They stood there, holding each other.

Winnie came out of Alma's bedroom and joined them. Mollie stood away from the group, but Callie put out an arm and brought the girl into the circle. Winnie spread her arms wide to encompass each of them.

Then Brenna started laughing. "I can't breathe."

Winnie giggled. "Okay, a little air here, ladies."

Alma backed up, but just a bit. "Winnie, say a prayer for us."

Winnie did just that, her Cajun French as melodious as a song. Alma didn't have to know all the words to understand the time-honored prayer. It was the twenty-third psalm.

He could hear the prayer inside his head.

Julien heard it as clearly as if someone was standing next to him. "The Lord is my shepherd; I shall not want."

He closed his eyes. His head hurt with all the brute force of two alligators fighting inside his brain. And one of them kept whipping Julien with his tail.

Then he opened his eyes and saw an egret flying through the cypress trees. Where in the world was he, anyway?

"Hey, bro, are you awake?"

Julien turned to see Tebow lying covered with

a tarp across from him in the speed boat. Then he remembered. They'd gotten caught in the storm. They'd been out with several other boats and the Coast Guard, looking for Pierre and Ramon Blanchard, but the thunder and lightning and wind had been too much. Too much. Tebow's speed boat had been tossed around like a spinning top.

And his friend had convinced him to pull up and wait it out in a hidden cove at the mouth of the pass into the big bay. A cove that, according to some of the old-timers, Ramon Blanchard liked to fish. Second Chance Landing.

"If your paw took de skiff, he'd want to test it in dat little hidden cove, Julien. Check dere first."

But they hadn't found the skiff. Or anyone here for that matter. They only found rushing water and an angry sky and a dark, dark dusk. A fool's errand. But Julien wouldn't give up.

Tebow sat up, his clothes damp and muddy. Pushing the dirty black tarp away, he said, "For sure, that was one of the worst tempests I've ever been through. Good thing we washed up here, rather than out in that bay, bro."

"The Coast Guard," Julien said, his throat dry. "We have to radio someone and find out where they are. The others might have gone home, but the Coast Guard should still be out in the bay searching." Or they may have called off the search.

"I'll try," Tebow said, shaking his head, his hand reaching for the radio. "Most everybody else went home after dark. Too messy to search."

But *they'd* stayed. Julien had insisted, even though they'd been forced to pull up here to wait out the storm.

Tebow hadn't put up a fight, but he kept shaking his head all the while.

Tebow put out a call to any nearby boaters, using the name of his boat, *Tebow's Treasure,* and their location inside what the locals called the Pass Cove.

The radio remained silent except for some static.

Then Julien heard a call. "Mayday, Mayday, Mayday. This is the LeBlanc skiff inside Pass Cove." The grainy voice named the coordinates. "I need help. Emergency. I need help."

Tebow and Julien both listened to the location. The other boat was about a mile south of them. Julien grabbed the radio handle from Tebow. "Pierre, this is your brother. Please respond."

Seven o'clock in the morning. Alma's skin crawled with raw nerves, her spine caught in a shivering tingle, her fingers shaking each time she tried to perform a task.

She stopped to stare out the café window. People arrived to begin the vigil. They brought sandwiches and drinks, Bibles and radios, cell phones and maps. She'd opened the café out of desire to stay busy, but everyone else took over the work.

People here knew they could come in, go behind the counter and fix whatever they wanted. Alma's mother Lila had taught her girls to make people feel welcome. Alma didn't have to lift a finger, so she just stood near the iris, now back in its place on the long counter. The bulb was sprouting new growth and the one open blossom was a silky, lush light purple.

She needed to plant the iris. She would. Soon. Very soon.

But now, each time she heard a phone ring, she jumped, stopped and listened. People came by, touching her hand, offering her a whisper and a prayer.

Dear Lord, please bring them home. Please bring them home.

She thought of having Julien at her door each morning and how she'd taken that for granted for so long now. She thought of her sweet papa and how she sometimes forgot to call and check on him. She thought of Callie and that mutt of a dog named Elvis. The mutt that had slept on her front porch all night without a whimper or a complaint. Keeping vigil. She thought of Brenna, heartbroken but here and taking charge. She watched as

Mrs. LeBlanc and Mrs. Laborde, Winnie and Mollie and the rest of the crew went about their work, silent and stoic, and she longed, oh, how she longed for the joy she always found here each morning.

She'd never find that kind of joy again if Julien didn't come back to her, if her papa and Pierre didn't... She couldn't think it. Wouldn't believe it.

God is good. Even when I'm hurting and in despair, God is good. But Dear Lord, some burdens are just too terrible to bear.

She only wanted to dance with Julien again. To dance and laugh and love him again. Why had it taken her so long to realize that?

Alma looked around, saw the love and the faith of her family and friends, saw the shining bond of these people and their traditions. And she remembered the words Jacob Sonnier had spoken to her the day before.

Why would you want to give up that quaint little café for some big-city chain restaurant? Trust me, it looks glamorous but it's a lot of hard work.

Hard work, she knew. Glamour, she didn't need.

She needed love and family and good food and...Julien.

Her dreams had been right here all along. She

could do anything she wanted to do right here in Fleur. With Julien by her side.

If only he'd come home to her.

"Over there!"

Tebow pointed to a copse of cypress trees so thick with gray moss they looked like a row of ghost soldiers with long gray beards. Knotted broken trunks and tangled roots surrounded the thicket, but Julien spotted the shattered wood of the skiff crammed like an angry fist against the mass of knotted "knees" that made up the white-washed trunks and limbs.

The skiff was broken and crushed against the unforgiving arms of the swamp thicket. But sitting up on top of one of the broken trunks was his brother Pierre. And lying unconscious across Pierre's lap was Ramon Blanchard.

Chapter Twenty

Ten in the morning

Alma took another headache pill and prayed another prayer.

The crowd had grown. People were milling around inside the café and out on the street and the back porch. Every few minutes someone would run in, saying they'd heard chatter on the radio. The Coast Guard helicopter had flown by about an hour ago.

But nothing since then.

The search party had gone back out with the Wildlife and Fishery agents and the sheriff's department and their own police chief. The Coast Guard was still out trolling the waters of the bay, too.

But Alma had work to keep her from falling to pieces.

She'd ordered the staff to cook as many hamburgers and fried catfish as they could so she could feed everyone. She had plenty of gumbo to sell or give away. She didn't want to charge, but people kept putting money in a Mason jar on the counter.

Why hadn't they heard anything more from all the boaters who'd gone back out at dawn? They'd heard rumors, false alarms, all sorts of tales, but no one had heard anything concrete.

Except that the boat carrying Julien and Tebow had not come home last night. Julien had stayed. He'd stayed for her father and his brother. Alma couldn't think beyond that. But she'd prayed herself into a tight little ball of calm. She wouldn't break; she wouldn't give up hope. Not yet. Not yet.

Julien had promised her he'd find her father and they'd both come back to her.

Whatever was going on out in that vast swamp and the surrounding sea, no one was saying. It could be good or it could be bad. The search party wouldn't confirm until they had something to report, no matter the chatter coming over the radios. They'd only come back with something factual and accurate—and final.

Her cell rang and she jumped so quickly she hit her knee on a bar stool. "Hello?"

"Alma, it's Jacob Sonnier. I think I've got some people interested in your gumbo."

Alma swallowed the bile back. She didn't want to think about this right now. This was Sunday. Didn't the man rest? "Uh, thank you, Mr. Sonnier. I'll have to get back to you. We've…we have an emergency going on right now. Some people are missing since the storm—"

She stopped, a hand going to her throat. Was she dreaming? Was this a nightmare? "My daddy is one of them." *And the man I love, the man I kept pushing away.*

"Oh, I'm so sorry," Mr. Sonnier replied. "What can I do to help?"

Alma wanted to shout at the man and tell him he could go out there and find the people she loved. But she didn't say that. "Just pray. I'll call you after I hear something."

He hung up with the promise to drive back to Fleur instead of heading back to I-10. He wanted to do whatever he could before he headed back to Georgia.

A nice sentiment, but what could he do? What could any of them do?

Reverend Guidry came up to the counter. "Alma, it's time for church. Since we have so many here, we thought we'd have it out under the big tent. The sun is shining again." His eyes held that same hope she'd seen in Virginia LeBlanc's eyes. How did they stay so strong? Why didn't they call out to God the way she wanted to?

"Alma?"

Alma nodded. "I'll be right there."

Maybe going to worship would calm her well-hidden nerves, stop the thudding beat of her erratic heart. She needed something to center her and give her the courage to keep going until she knew one way or another if they were all safe.

Callie took Alma's hand on one side and Brenna tugged her arm against Alma's on the other. Together, they walked over to the church parking lot, where the big red-and-white-striped tent shined brightly against the fresh sunshine. The tent had been tossed and rearranged, but some of the men had hammered down the big stakes and tightened the ropes and cables to secure it back in place. A few rips allowed sun rays to prance across the asphalt, and all around tree limbs and tossed folding chairs lay scattered like trash from a giant can.

The church members and all the others gathered and silently found the chairs and brought them back underneath the tent. Soon the event, haphazard and quickly arranged, became a silent and somber meeting of hundreds of anxious, worried people.

Reverend Guidry waited until everyone had found a seat, then he began to pray. He asked the Lord to provide, no matter the day, no matter the need. He asked that God give strength to those waiting to hear about their loved ones.

"Comfort those waiting here, Lord. Bring Alma and her sisters, Callie and Brenna, the peace beyond understanding. Bring their beloved daddy back safe. Help Mrs. LeBlanc and sustain her until she knows the fate of her two sons, Julien and Pierre. Help Mrs. Laborde and her son Tebow, who went out to help a friend. Help all of us, Lord, to understand the ways of nature, but please, Lord, help those out there searching. Bring our loved ones back to us."

Alma followed the prayer, waiting, hoping, sending up her own promises and pleas.

After the prayer ended, she glanced over at Mrs. LeBlanc. Virginia's smile was bittersweet, but it still held that radiant hope Alma had seen last night. She smiled at Julien's mother, then blinked back the tears she refused to cry. She could be strong. She'd been strong during her mother's illness and death. She'd been strong when she made the decision to stay here with her daddy and Callie. She'd be strong now, while she waited and wondered and prayed for Julien and the others to come back.

Reverend Guidry suggested a hymn.

And so they sang "Peace Like A River," at first without instruments or an organ, but then someone stepped up with a fiddle and the soft notes hit the air with a sweet intensity. The music, low and full of praise, lifted over the trees and drowned out the slow Sunday traffic.

Then Mollie stepped up to stand with the fiddler and she began to sing the lyrics in Cajun French. *Paix comme une rivière dans mon âme…*

"I've got peace like a river in my soul."

Alma heard the simple words of peace, love and joy and she thought of the river and the bayou and the vast bay that lead to the ocean. This was her life, her water, her land. Her home.

But she couldn't stay here without Julien.

She closed her eyes and listened to Mollie's voice lifting out over the sky and asked God to show her some of that peace.

Julien watched as the Coast Guard chopper airlifted Mr. Blanchard out of the swamp. They were administering treatment and taking him to the nearby hospital. Pierre was with Julien and Tebow in Tebow's boat. He'd refused any further treatment beyond some water and being checked for vital signs.

From what Julien could tell, other than a few scrapes, bruises and bug bites, his brother was okay. But Ramon Blanchard had hit his head when the boat was tossed up into the marshes. He was still unconscious.

Pierre, unharmed physically, was beside himself. "He wouldn't let me go out there by myself, bro. He knew I'd been drinking but he got in that boat and he refused to leave me." He wiped at his red eyes. "Mr. Blanchard told me about how much it hurt to lose his wife, Miss Lila. He sat there and he cried. Then I cried out there in the wind and the rain. Then the storm got worse and we held on. We held on." He stared at the chopper. "He can't die, Julien. He saved my life. He was trying to get us back home."

Julien's heart opened wide for the man who'd scowled at him for most of his life. Mr. Blanchard had probably saved Pierre's life in more ways than one.

After they'd called the emergency alert, two Louisiana Department of Wildlife and Fisheries boats had responded, followed by a Coast Guard helicopter. The helicopter had sent down a medic and a stretcher.

Now Julien had to get back to Fleur and tell Alma her father was still alive. The search party was over. The LDWF officers were escorting them home.

Home.

Home and into Alma's arms.

But would she forgive him if her father didn't make it?

Would she forgive him for being a dolt and

silently accusing her of the very thing he'd feared for most of his life?

That she'd leave him?

Why did you wait ten long years to win her back then lose her all over again?

Julien had no answers for the many questions flowing like the current inside his tired brain. He only knew he wanted to be in Alma's arms again. Forever.

So he braced himself against the wind and the currents and he held on while the men who'd helped rescue them taxied him back to the people he loved.

She heard the helicopter's heavy hover over the sound of the fiddle. Alma stopped singing and ran out from under the tent to stare up into the sky, her hands shielding her eyes.

"The Coast Guard," she shouted, tears forming in her eyes.

Then everyone started talking at once.

"They found 'em," one man shouted. "Not sure what kind of condition."

Callie and Brenna stood with her, watching until the helicopter disappeared over the treeline.

"They could be headed to the hospital," Brenna said. "Or they might be taking someone to a bigger hospital in New Orleans."

"But who?" Alma's heart sat frozen in place. She couldn't find her next breath.

Ignoring the shouts coming from inside the tent, she started walking toward the marina. Then before she knew it, she was running, running toward the water.

She heard motors humming as the flotilla of search boats started returning to the docks. Alma strained to see if Tebow's boat or the skiff were among them. She didn't see either.

Behind her, she heard footsteps and saw that the crowd from the worship service had made its way to the marina, too.

Her sisters caught up with her and stood nearby, waiting. She felt the collective breath of the whole town, holding, waiting, wondering what had happened. And who had survived.

And then she heard the roar of another motor and saw the LDWF agents escorting one more boat into the marina.

Tebow's battered speed boat.

And three men were on that boat.

Alma gulped in air, swallowed a sob. One of the men was Julien.

"I don't see Daddy," Brenna said. "Alma, where is Papa?"

Alma couldn't stop the tears then. Julien was alive. Pierre was with him and so was Tebow. But where was her daddy?

* * *

Julien searched the marina and spotted Alma there apart from the rest of the crowd, wearing jeans and a blue cotton top. Her hair was down and flowing around her face, the wind lifting it like a silky scarf.

He got out of the boat and hurried to her. She moved toward him, hurrying, running, until he could hear her flip-flops hitting the weathered boards of the boardwalk. Julien started running, too, his tiredness gone now, his pulse pumping new life with each beat of her footsteps.

And then he had her in his arms and he was holding her tight and kissing her hair. He murmured words, long held and long thought, in her ear. *"Je suis désolé, chère. Désolé. Je t'aime. Je t'aime toujours."*

Alma lifted her head, her eyes holding his. "Why are you sorry, Julien? Where is my papa? Please tell me the truth? Is he still alive?"

Julien hated the pain and fear he saw in her eyes. Had she heard him tell her how much he loved her? *"Oui,* he's alive."

"But that was him, on the chopper?"

"Yes. I'll take you to the hospital."

He let her go when he saw Pierre hugging their mother. Julien did the same. "I'm okay, *Maman.* We're both all right." Then he explained about Ramon Blanchard. "He…he went with Pierre, to help the boy. To talk to him. Mr. Blanchard was driving the boat the whole time."

People came running before he could finish.

"I'm fine, everyone. Tebow can fill y'all in on the rest. Now I need to get Alma and her sisters to the Fleur Medical Center to see how her daddy's doing."

Alma sat in the waiting room, holding a cold cup of bad coffee. "Why haven't we heard something?"

Brenna and Callie sat nearby. "They have to stabilize him," Brenna explained. "You heard the intern."

"I heard, but I want to see him," Alma replied.

She glanced up to where Julien stood staring out a big window. Putting down the coffee, she went to him, her arm touching his dirty shirt. "Julien, we can get you some clean clothes."

He tugged her close. "I'm okay. I don't want to leave you. Besides, if I know my mama, she'll be here soon with clothes and food." Kissing her hair, he said, "I'm just glad to be with you again."

Alma leaned into him, the smell of mud and the bayou as much a part of him as the scent of spice she usually associated with him. "Julien, about yesterday…"

"Hush, hush," he said, a finger to her lips. "Remember that old saying, 'Where there is love, there is forgiveness,' *oui?*" Then he leaned down to kiss her. "Can you forgive me?"

"Nothing to forgive," Alma said. "I just wanted you to know—I'm not leaving Fleur, ever."

Julien pulled back to stare at her. "Now, don't go making any rash decisions. I was wrong to assume you'd be leaving anyway. I only heard what I feared, *catin.*"

"And I only saw what I thought I wanted," she replied. "If I ever talk to Mr. Sonnier again, it will be about packaging some of my dishes for distribution, nothing more. Except maybe a cookbook. Things I can do right here."

Julien's eyes shined brightly with pride. "There you go. You can do that, Alma. You owe it to the world, all the wonderful food you cook."

"And you could live with that?"

"I told you, I love you. I can live with anything as long as I know you love me back."

Alma saw the questions on his eyes, but before she could answer, the doors to the emergency room opened and two doctors came walking toward them.

"Julien?"

"I'm right here," he said, turning her toward her sisters and the doctors.

Alma gathered with her family, holding tight to her sisters and to Julien. "How is he?" she asked.

"He's a lucky man," the intern said. "He has a

concussion but it's a mild one. He just needs to rest and take it easy for the next few days. His vitals are good and his heartbeat is strong. Your daddy is one stubborn man. He told us he's survived worse than this, many times."

"That's true," Callie said, tears streaming down her face. "He is tough."

"He's asking for all of you," the doctor said. "Oh, and he especially asked for Julien."

"That's me," Julien said, giving Alma a blank stare.

After the doctor left, they started toward the emergency room. "I guess he's gonna tell me to get lost since my baby brother just about killed him."

"It's okay," Alma said. But she couldn't predict what her father might have to say.

They all went behind the curtain separating her daddy from the other patient who shared the room. "Daddy," she exclaimed, running to hug her father close. His bear hug proved that he was as strong as ever.

After more hugs, tears and laughter, he finally looked up at Julien. "And you—"

"I'm so sorry," Julien began, his hands palm up. "Pierre shouldn't have taken that boat out in that storm."

"I asked your brother to take it for a spin," Ramon said. "I made him let me take over once we got out there, but I wasn't gonna let that boy get on that boat by himself and drink, no sir. Turns out, we had a right fine discussion."

"You could have been killed," Brenna said, glaring over at Julien.

"But I'm here," Ramon replied. "Before… before the storm hit, Pierre and I had a long talk. I think he'll straighten up just fine. I told him about my own grief." He stopped, his eyes misty. "Then I told him if his brother marries my daughter, he'd be part of our family. And our family expects more outta a person." He grinned, winced, then said, "I wasn't completely passed out after I hit my head. I heard that boy apologize to me so many times, I had to take me a little nap. And dat was dat."

Alma saw Julien's broad smile. Then her father held up a beefy hand. "But, son, your skiff is… gone."

"I saw that," Julien replied, shaking his head. "I'll build another one, even better."

"I'll help you," Ramon said, nodding. "Now dat you for sure gonna be my son-in-law."

Julien turned to Alma then. "Will you…marry me, that is?"

Alma's heart opened wide as a warmth and understanding moved through her. "Yes."

More tears. More hugs. More promises to be honored.

Soon a nurse came in and told them Mr. Blanchard would be moved to a room for overnight observation. They all piled out into the waiting room.

Jacob Sonnier was waiting for them. "How's your daddy?"

Alma explained what had happened. "He should be just fine."

"That's good," the older man said. "Just wanted to check."

Alma glanced at Julien then turned back to Jacob. "I think I'd like to take you up on that offer to distribute my gumbo, Mr. Sonnier."

"Really?"

She nodded. "Just give me some time to get things in order." Then she grinned and pointed toward Julien. "Starting with my wedding."

Mr. Sonnier let out a hoot of laughter. "Son, you'll be marrying one very smart businesswoman."

Julien kissed her forehead. "I couldn't agree more."

A few minutes later, Julien's mother and Pierre, followed by Tebow and Mollie and Mrs. Laborde, came charging in with food and clean clothes. Mrs. LeBlanc had brought enough to feed the entire emergency room staff. "Reverend Guidry says the street dance is back on tonight," she announced.

Jacob Sonnier took it all in. "Ain't that good?"

"Very good," Julien said in Alma's ear.

She turned to stare up at him. "I love you, too," she said.

Julien kissed her again. *"Veux-tu danser avec moi?"*

"Yes, I'll dance with you. Tonight," she promised.

A few hours later, a slow song drifted out onto the night, its notes touching the stars while the only couple left on the dance floor gently swayed to the music.

Julien held Alma close, taking in the scent of flowers surrounding her soft, long hair. "We're gonna be okay, aren't we, *chère?*"

"Better than okay," she replied.

"No regrets?"

"No regrets," she said. "I have everything I've ever wanted, right here in Fleur."

"Why did we wait so long?"

Alma glanced up at him, her eyes warm and bright. "God's own time, Julien. We had to have this reunion to appreciate how deeply our love runs."

He held her face in his hands, amazed that she was his at last. "A sweetheart reunion. This time, I won't let you go."

Alma kissed him then giggled. "I think this is why I never left in the first place."

The music stopped, but Julien held her there. This was one dance that would last a lifetime. He had his Alma back, at long last.

* * * * *

Dear Reader,

I love reunion stories. I think I appreciate these stories because they show us that we always have a second chance. Alma and Julien had this second chance after many years of trying hard to ignore each other. When Julien had his epiphany, he knew it was a sign from God that he needed to settle down. He wanted to do that but not without Alma.

I hope you enjoyed watching Alma and Julien rekindle their love. I purposely set this story in south Louisiana, near the Gulf Coast, because I love the resilience of the people in that particular part of the state. They are strong and hardworking and durable. They have survived storms and heartache, but they always bounce back. I believe God gave us the ultimate reunion story when he sent Christ to be the buffer in our reunion with him. We always have a second chance to be reunited with someone we love, thanks to the love of Christ.

Until next time, may the angels watch over you always.

Lenora Worth

Questions For Discussion

1. It took Julien many years to realize he wanted to win Alma back. Why do you think it took him so long?

2. Have you ever wanted to reunite with a loved one or a friend but were afraid to take that first step? Did this story help you with that?

3. Why do you think people grow apart? Can being a Christian help you deal with losing a loved one in anger?

4. Why did Alma hold back from accepting Julien's love? Do you think her worries about getting sick like her mother were valid?

5. Have you ever had to deal with the death of a loved one from cancer? If so, how have you learned to cope?

6. Alma comes from a strong, close-knit family. Did this help her or hinder her in dealing with Julien's love?

7. Why did Alma wait before planting the iris Julien gave her?

8. Julien wanted to help his brother, Pierre. Have you ever had to deal with a loved one who is in trouble in this way? How did you handle that situation?

9. Do you think Pierre was acting out because of watching Julien do the same? Or maybe because he missed his father?

10. Alma and Julien live in an area hit hard by both nature and life in general. Do you find this to be realistic compared to today's world?

11. Fleur is a small community where everyone comes together to help each other. Do you live in such a community? Have you found that this type of community helps you in your faith?

12. Why do you think Ramon Blanchard got on the boat with Pierre?

13. Do you think Pierre will straighten up and make a life with Pretty Mollie? Should she stick by him?

14. Alma wanted a career and to marry Julien. Why was it so hard for her to accept that she can have both? Do you believe she can have both?

15. Why was Julien so afraid of letting Alma spread her wings? Do you believe couples can compromise and still have a solid marriage?

LARGER-PRINT BOOKS!

GET 2 FREE
LARGER-PRINT NOVELS
PLUS 2 FREE
MYSTERY GIFTS

Love Inspired®

Larger-print novels are now available...

YES! Please send me 2 FREE LARGER-PRINT Love Inspired® novels and my 2 FREE mystery gifts (gifts are worth about $10). After receiving them, if I don't wish to receive any more books, I can return the shipping statement marked "cancel". If I don't cancel, I will receive 6 brand-new novels every month and be billed just $4.99 per book in the U.S. or $5.49 per book in Canada. That's a saving of at least 23% off the cover price. It's quite a bargain! Shipping and handling is just 50¢ per book in the U.S. and 75¢ per book in Canada.* I understand that accepting the 2 free books and gifts places me under no obligation to buy anything. I can always return a shipment and cancel at any time. Even if I never buy another book, the two free books and gifts are mine to keep forever.

122/322 IDN FEG3

Name _____ (PLEASE PRINT) _____

Address _____ Apt. # _____

City _____ State/Prov. _____ Zip/Postal Code _____

Signature (if under 18, a parent or guardian must sign) _____

Mail to the **Reader Service:**
IN U.S.A.: P.O. Box 1867, Buffalo, NY 14240-1867
IN CANADA: P.O. Box 609, Fort Erie, Ontario L2A 5X3

Not valid to current subscribers to Love Inspired Larger-Print books.

**Are you a current subscriber to Love Inspired books
and want to receive the larger-print edition?
Call 1-800-873-8635 or visit www.ReaderService.com.**

* Terms and prices subject to change without notice. Prices do not include applicable taxes. Sales tax applicable in N.Y. Canadian residents will be charged applicable taxes. Offer not valid in Quebec. This offer is limited to one order per household. All orders subject to credit approval. Credit or debit balances in a customer's account(s) may be offset by any other outstanding balance owed by or to the customer. Please allow 4 to 6 weeks for delivery. Offer available while quantities last.

Your Privacy—The Reader Service is committed to protecting your privacy. Our Privacy Policy is available online at www.ReaderService.com or upon request from the Reader Service.

We make a portion of our mailing list available to reputable third parties that offer products we believe may interest you. If you prefer that we not exchange your name with third parties, or if you wish to clarify or modify your communication preferences, please visit us at www.ReaderService.com/consumerchoice or write to us at Reader Service Preference Service, P.O. Box 9062, Buffalo, NY 14269. Include your complete name and address.

LILP11B

Love Inspired SUSPENSE

RIVETING INSPIRATIONAL ROMANCE

Watch for our series of edge-
of-your-seat suspense novels.
These contemporary tales
of intrigue and romance
feature Christian characters
facing challenges to their faith...
and their lives!

AVAILABLE IN REGULAR
& LARGER-PRINT FORMATS

For exciting stories that reflect traditional values,
visit:
www.ReaderService.com

LISUSDIR118

Reader Service.com

You can now manage your account online!

- Review your order history
- Manage your payments
- Update your address

We've redesigned the Reader Service website just for you.

Now you can:

- Read excerpts
- Respond to mailings and special monthly offers
- Learn about new series available to you

Visit us today:

www.ReaderService.com

RS10